"Your New Wardrobe Is In The Plane. There's A Room In The Back. *Change.*"

Of all the high-handedness, of all the *arrogance!* Of all the bosses in the world—she had to be in debt to *Marcos.*

While the jet motors hummed in the background, Virginia slipped into the slinky patterned dress inside the windowless little room at the back of the plane. The clothes were divine. She couldn't in her right mind stay annoyed at a man with such exquisite taste. Her knight in shining armor.

Enthralled by how slight and satiny the dress felt against her body, she ran three fingers down the length of her hips, wishing there were a mirror to visually appreciate its exquisite plunging back. *And how is this necessary to his plan?* she wondered.

Gathering her courage with a steady inhale, she forced herself to step outside.

And there was nothing to pry his glimmering eyes away from her, no shield from the scorching possessiveness flickering in their depths....

Dear Reader,

This book, my first Desire, was an adventure to write. Adventure in the sense of me, being immersed in this wonderful story, bravely struggling to adjust my vision to something that would do justice to the wonderfully provocative Desire line. Believe me when I say this was no easy feat when you start with a stubborn hero like mine!

Marcos is a ruthless man, and so stubborn he wouldn't bend to my ideas no matter what I did or said. He always won. Powerful in character and in will—he's determined to get what he wants and he always gets his way. But despite the constant headaches from the man, I realized there was always one constant in him. No matter what he did, or where he was, or what I demanded that he do, Marcos wanted Virginia with a passion. A passion that could make *any* woman, even this author, tremble.

As I wrote, I learned to see our heroine, his lovely assistant Virginia, through his eyes. And boy, how I grew to admire Virginia's quiet strength! Just to work for her powerful boss and remain sane seems like a Herculean task. And where I, author and supposed master of this story, failed to domesticate our billionaire hero, Virginia succeeded with her quiet loyalty and determination to get ahead in life.

Her boss wants her. He always has. He wants her bad enough to help her, bad enough to bend for her. He wants her bad enough that, this time, Marcos Allende will get more than he bargained for.

Enjoy,

Red Garnier

RED GARNIER

THE SECRETARY'S BOSSMAN BARGAIN

Published by Silhouette Books
America's Publisher of Contemporary Romance

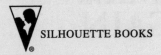 SILHOUETTE BOOKS

ISBN-13: 978-0-373-73041-4

THE SECRETARY'S BOSSMAN BARGAIN

Recycling programs
for this product may
not exist in your area.

RED GARNIER

is a fan of books, chocolate and happily ever afters. What better way to spend the day than combining all three? Traveling frequently between the United States and Mexico, Red likes to call Texas home. She'd love to hear from her readers at redgarnier@gmail.com. For more on upcoming books and current contests, please visit her Web site, www.redgarnier.com.

This book is dedicated to the fabulous Desire editors,
who provide endless wisdom, advice and inspiration.
Krista, Charles, and Shana—
Thank you for the gift of writing for your line.

And to Diana Ventimiglia,
who believed in me since the beginning.
You're fondly remembered.

One

She was ready to beg him.

Virginia Hollis shuddered. She wrapped her arms around herself and stared out the back window of the sleek black Lincoln as it wound along the darkened streets of Chicago. People strolled down the block, hands in their pockets, chins neatly tucked to their chests to shield their faces from the biting wind. Men held cell phones to their ears; women struggled with their shopping bags. One glimpse made it seem like such a regular evening. An ordinary night.

But it wasn't ordinary. It couldn't be.

Because Virginia's world had stopped turning.

The men who'd knocked on her door this morning had had a message for her, and it had not been a kind one.

She inhaled deeply and glanced at her simple black dress and the delicate strappy heels on her pink-toed feet. It seemed important for her to look nice—not just respectable, but sophisticated, noble—because the favor she was to ask was anything but.

And she could think of no one else to ask but *him*. God. Just thinking of humiliating herself like this in front of *him* made her stomach churn.

Nervously, she tugged on the pearl strand draped around her neck and tried focusing on the city again. The pearls were smooth under her fingers, genuine and old, the only thing Virginia had been able to salvage from her mother's belongings.

Her father had lost it all.

Bet by bet, he'd lost the cars, the antiques, the house. Virginia had watched with a combination of helplessness and rage. She'd threatened, screamed, pleaded with the quickly aging man, all to no avail.

There was no stopping him. No stopping the gambling.

There was nothing left now.

Nothing but her.

And she could not, *could* not, turn a blind eye to those men—to the threat they posed. To the threat they had succinctly delivered. No matter how much she frowned upon what her father did, and no matter how many times she'd promised never again to speak to him about it and he continued gambling anyway, he was her father. Her only family.

Once he'd been a businessman. Respected, admired even. Now it saddened her to think what she'd become.

Virginia didn't know how much he owed. She'd rather not know. All she knew was the deal she'd struck with those three surly men that morning. She had a month to come up with one hundred thousand dollars, during which time they would leave him alone.

In her wildest dreams, Virginia had never imagined coming up with that amount of money, on such little time. But while *she* couldn't, Marcos Allende could.

The little hairs on her arms pricked to attention at the thought of him. Her boss was a quiet, devastatingly handsome man. Some said he was gifted; his touch was that of a Midas. While Virginia had only been his assistant for a year—his third of three assistants, because it seemed one alone couldn't handle the daunting task of having him as boss—in that length of time, she had seen enough of him to agree.

The man was out of context.

He was bold, ruthless and proud. Single-handedly, he'd spotted, bought and righted troubled companies, and he'd created an empire. He inspired respect and admiration among peers and fear among his enemies. Judging by the overwhelming number of phone calls he received from the female population of Chicago, Virginia could tell they adored him. And in Virginia herself, the man inspired things she dared not consider.

Every morning when she stepped into his office, he would study her with that dark, compelling gaze and disturb every inch and atom of her body with the hot intimacy in his eyes. She would always try to act professionally, to look away when his stare became inappropriately long. But his eyes had a way of undressing her, of speaking in silence, of summoning visions in her mind about him and her and skin and sweat. Yet tonight she was on her way to him for one purpose only, and she reminded herself that her visit to his lair at such a late hour might not be welcome.

With his assistants he was always the firm, quiet boss, but Marcos Allende was reputed to have a hell of a temper, one she might witness tonight for the very first time.

Her stomach clenched when the car pulled into the ample driveway of one of the Windy City's most luxurious apartment buildings, situated on the heavily trafficked Michigan Avenue. A uniformed valet opened the door.

She mumbled a quick "thank you" and stepped out of the car, walking into the sumptuous apartment building with an eerie calm that belied every one of the roiling emotions inside her.

She made no eye contact with the people milling around the area, but instead focused all of her attention on the polished bronze doors at the far end of the lobby.

"Mr. Allende is expecting you."

An elevator attendant waited for her. He slipped a card into the top slot inside the confined elevator space and lit the top *P* before stepping out with a bow. "Good evening, madam."

The doors closed and Virginia stared at her blurry reflection.

Oh, God, please let him help me. I'll do anything. Anything...

Long seconds later, the doors rolled open to reveal the penthouse—a vast room with black granite floors, dimly lit and lavishly furnished. The walls could've been covered in crisp green bills and screamed the owner's net worth just as loudly. To a mortal, his place seemed as inaccessible in price as the owner was claimed to be in character.

Virginia stepped inside. A pair of elegant, willowy bronzes flanked the entry and a massive oil painting with vibrant black brushstrokes hung at the end wall. Before she could absorb the rest of the opulent area, as though drawn by some unknown force of nature, her gaze landed on him. He stood next to the bar at the far end of the living room. He was as elegant and unmoving as the designer furniture surrounding him. Dark, tall, detached. He faced the window, his broad back filling the shoulders of his jacket. Her heart thumped as she took a step forward, the click of her heels on granite magnified in the silence.

"I trust you had a fine ride."

Her flesh pebbled at the hum of his voice. So husky. So mellow. As though he were no threat to anyone. The crackling energy around him dispelled the notion fast.

"I did. Thank you for sending a car, and for seeing me on such short notice," she said quietly.

Starting to shake inside, she advanced toward the living room, stepping lightly across a plush Persian rug. He didn't turn. Virginia wasn't certain she even wanted him to. Every time their gazes met, a bolt of electricity would shoot through her. Sometimes he didn't even need to speak. His eyes did it for him. And in her mind, he said the wickedest things to her.

Now here she was, in his apartment, ready to face that bold, virile man she'd fantasized about. Ready to beg him.

Never mind Virginia had her modestly successful life, which she'd tried to live by the book. Never mind she'd paid her bills on time and tried first and foremost to stay out of trouble. Never mind anything but what had to be done. Saving her father. Doing anything she had to, to make him safe again.

She could've sworn Marcos read her thoughts just now, for he whispered, "Are you in trouble, Virginia?" While still gazing out the window as though mesmerized by the tiny flicker of city lights.

She swallowed, eyeing his back. "It appears I am."

"And you came to ask for my help?"

A ball of unease settled in the pit of her stomach, and the words seemed to be wrenched from her throat. "I do need your help, Marcos."

He turned, and she was rendered motionless by the sheer black power of his stare. "How much?"

Her heart pounded faster. His face was so exquisitely masculine, and there was something so naughty about him—his attitude, his dark good looks, his accent—that a dormant part of her found thrilling and frightening at once. Every inch of his Latin blood showed in his bronzed skin, the very masculinity oozing from his pores.

His inquisitive gaze traveled with interest down the length of her body until she could bear no more. She lifted her chin with pride, though the way she wrung her hands before her wasn't all that convincing. "I—I don't expect anything for free. I wanted to see you about an advance. A loan. Perhaps I could do more work for you. Special projects."

His eyelids dropped as he sighted her lips. "You're very pretty tonight, Virginia."

The low seduction in his words made her heart clench in a fistful of thrill. She fought the thrill, telling herself he was a sexy, virile man—and that he must look at all women this way. Which was why they called him. All. The. Time! When those eyes were on her, he made her feel like the sexiest woman alive—like the only woman alive.

"I'm trying to raise…" She paused, summoning all her courage. "I'm trying to raise one hundred thousand dollars. Can you help me?" she asked him then, lowering her face. As she spoke, she felt so…so cheap…so humiliated to be asking for money…

"Is that all you need?" he asked softly. As though it were nothing. A paltry sum. And to him, with all his billions, of course it would be.

He surveyed her in silence. "May I ask why you need it?"

Her gaze flicked up to his, and she shook her head. She couldn't bear it.

His lips twitched and the corners of his eyes crinkled, almost—*almost*—managing to make him less threatening. "You won't tell me?" he prodded.

"If you don't mind," she mumbled. She tugged the hem of her dress to her knees when his gaze ventured to her legs and lingered. "So there's nothing I could do for you? In exchange for this…incredible salary?" God. She couldn't even say the amount it seemed so out of reach.

He laughed, and Virginia didn't think she'd ever heard him laugh before. The sound resembled the roll of distant thunder.

He set his glass on the nearby bar and signaled to the twin leather couches. "Sit."

She sat. Her back was stiff and straight as she tracked his lithe moves around the room. How could a big man move with such grace? How could—

"Wine?"

"No."

He poured two glasses nonetheless. His hands moved skillfully—too skillfully not to notice—and brought one to her.

"Drink."

She grasped the fluted glass and stared at a faraway bronze sculpture, trying not to breathe for fear of what his scent might do to her. He smelled so amazingly good. Earthy and musky and male. She drew in a shaky breath until he dropped onto the couch across from hers.

When he stretched his arms out behind him, he made the couch appear small, his wide frame overwhelming the bone-colored leather designer piece. Under his jacket, the dress shirt he wore was unbuttoned at the top, gifting her with a view of smooth, bronzed skin and a polished gold cross.

She wanted to touch him. She wondered what that bronze skin would feel like under her fingers, if his cross was cold or warm…

Suddenly sensing his scrutiny, she raised her chin and smiled.

Lifting one black brow, Marcos opened his hand and signaled to her. "You're not drinking."

Virginia started, then obediently sipped. "It's…good. Very…um, rich."

"Have I ever bitten you?"

She almost choked on the wine, blinked, and then, then she saw the smile. A prime smile. Rare, like everything valuable, higher on one end than the other.

"I can see this is difficult for you," he said, with a glimmer of warmth in his eyes.

"No. I mean, yes. It is." He had no clue!

He set his glass aside, crossed his arms over his chest, and snuggled back as if to watch a movie. "You don't trust me?"

Her heart skipped a nervous beat.

Trust him? She respected him. Admired him. Was in awe of him and, because of his power, even a little afraid of him. And maybe, she realized, she trusted him, too. From what she'd seen, Marcos—quiet, solid, heart-of-gold Marcos—had proved to be nothing but a champion for his people. A lion protecting his cubs. When Lindsay, assistant two, had been weeping for months after her twins were born, Marcos had hired an army of nannies and sent her off to a second honeymoon in Hawaii with her husband.

Lindsay was still talking about Maui.

And when Mrs. Fuller's husband passed away, the over-wrought woman had cried more tears reminiscing about all that Marcos had done to support and aid her family than she had cried at the funeral.

No matter how humiliating this was, how awful her situation and having him know it, she knew, like nothing in her life, he was as steady as a mountain.

Holding his gaze, she replied in all honesty. "I trust you more than I trust anyone."

His face lit in surprise, and he scraped his chin between two blunt fingers. "And yet you don't tell me what troubles you?"

The thought that he—the man she most honored, esteemed—would know her life was in such shambles squished her heart like a bug. "I would tell you what I need the money for if I thought it mattered, and I would tell you if that is the only way you'll give it to me."

With an expression that would befit a lone hunting wolf,

Marcos rose and strode over, then pried the glass from her fingers. "Come with me."

Unnerved that she couldn't even begin to guess the thoughts in that unique, labyrinthine mind of his, Virginia followed him down the wide, domed hallway of his penthouse, becoming acutely aware of his formidable frame next to her.

And she couldn't help but wonder if maybe she wasn't a little bit the fool for trusting him after all.

Predatorily, Marcos studied her profile, her nose, the untamed, unruly bounce of her curls. She bit her lip in nervousness. Where was he taking her?

Visions of a bedroom flicked across her mind, and her cheeks flamed hot.

He opened the last door for her, and Virginia entered the darkened room, shamed at her own quickening pulse.

"Your home office?" she asked.

"Yes."

He flicked on the light switch, and the room burst to life. Bookshelves lined three of the four walls. A Turkish rug spread across the sitting area. Five glossy wood file cabinets formed a long, neat row behind his desk. No adornments. No picture frames. No distractions. As fine in taste as the rest of his apartment, with a state-of-the-art computer perched atop a massive desk, his office screamed two words: *no nonsense*.

"I like it." She strode inside, the knowledge that this was his private, personal space making her blood bubble. Her fingers itched with the overwhelming urge to organize the stacks of papers on his desk.

"I know about your father, Miss Hollis."

Dread sunk like a bowling ball in her stomach. "You do?"

She spun around, and when he stepped into the room, Marcos achieved the impossible: he made it shrink in size.

"You do not exist in the world I do without being cautious about everyone who comes into your inner circle. I have a dossier on everyone who works in close proximity with me, and I know every detail of their lives. Yes, I know about his problem."

"Oh."

What else did he know?

He passed her as he crossed the room, and she stifled a tremor as if he'd been a cool hurricane wind. "Why didn't you come to me before?" he asked, matter of fact.

"I'm here now," she whispered.

Halting behind his desk, he shoved the leather chair aside and leaned over the surface. His shirt stretched taut over his bunched shoulders and his eyebrows pulled low. "How bad is it?"

"It... The gambling comes and goes." Flushing at his scrutiny, she turned to busy herself with the books on the shelves, and then said, as if he'd expertly unlatched a closed door which had been near bursting with secrets, "He's out of control. He keeps betting more than what he has and more than I could possibly earn."

"Is that the only reason you're here?"

His voice grew so textured, a jolt of feminine heat rippled through her. She spun around—shocked by the question. Shocked by the answering flutter in her womb.

Her breath stopped.

His gaze. It was open. Raw. Revealed a galvanizing wildness, a primitive hunger lurking—lurking *there*—in the depths of his eyes, like a prowling beast.

Pent-up desire rushed through her bloodstream as he continued to stare. Stare at her in a way no man, ever, should look at a woman and expect her to survive. "Is that the only reason you're here tonight? Virginia?"

As if in a trance, she moved forward on shaky legs, closer to his desk. "Y-yes."

"You want nothing else? Just the money?"

How to talk? How to think? Breathe? Her heart felt ready to pop from the pressure of answering. "N-nothing."

In the back of her mind, she vaguely realized how simple and unassuming her needs sounded as she voiced them. When they were not. They were tangled. They had grown fierce with his proximity. Out of reason, out of context, out of *control*.

"Will you help me," she murmured as she reached the desk, and somehow the plea sounded as intimate as if she'd asked for a kiss.

"I will." Deep and rough, the determination in his answer flooded her with relief.

He was going to help her.

In her soaring mind, Marcos was mounted on a white charger holding up a flag that read "Virginia."

And she…well, hers might be a banner. A neon sign. A brand on every inch of her body and possibly her heart. Marcos Allende. God, she was a fool.

"I don't expect something for nothing," she said. Her voice throbbed even as a tide of relief flooded her.

It was as if some unnatural force drew her to him, pulled her to get closer and closer. Did the force come from him? From her? If it weren't for the desk—always the desk between them—where would she be?

No. The obstacle wasn't a desk. It was everything. Everything. Nothing she could ever arrange or fix or clean.

Marcos raked one hand through his hair, then seized a runaway pen and thrust it into an empty leather holder. "I'll give you the money. But I have a few requests of my own."

"Anything," she said.

His gaze was positively lethal. His hands—they made fists. "There's something I want. Something that *belongs* to me. Something I must have or I'll lose my mind with wanting it."

A shiver ran hot and cold down her spine.

He wasn't speaking of her—of course he wasn't—but nonetheless, she felt something grip inside her as though he were. What would it feel like for Marcos to want her so fiercely? "I...understand."

"Do you?"

He smiled bleakly at her, then continued around his desk.

He swept up a gemstone globe from the edge and spun it around, a lapis lazuli ocean going round and round. "Here." His finger stopped the motion, marking a country encrusted in granite for her eyes. "What I want is here." He tapped.

Tap tap tap.

She stepped closer, longingly lifting a fingertip to stroke the length of the country he signaled. Travel had seemed so far down the line of her priorities she hardly gave any thought to it now.

"Mexico," she whispered.

His finger slid. It touched hers. He watched. And she watched. And neither of them moved. His finger was blunt and tan, hers slim and milky. Both over Mexico. It wasn't even a touch, not even half a touch. And she felt the contact in every fiber of her lonely, quivering being.

He turned his head, their faces so close that his pupils looked enormously black to her. A swirling vortex. He whispered, as though confessing his every hidden desire and sin, "I'm after Allende."

She connected the name immediately. "Your father's business?"

"The business he lost."

He set down the globe, and again, his finger. This time the back of it stroked down her cheek. Marcos touching her, Marcos looking so strangely at her, oh, God. He smelled so good she felt lightheaded.

"And you believe I can help?" she asked, one step away

from him, then two. Away from his magnificent, compelling force, away from what he made her want.

He scraped a restless hand down his face. "The owner has managed it poorly and contacted me for help." A tiny muscle ticked at the back of his jaw. "I'm usually a sucker for the ailing, I admit, but things are different in this case." Disgusted, he shook his head. "I do not intend to help her, you understand?"

"Yes." She didn't understand, exactly, but rumors around the office were that *no one* mentioned Allende to Marcos unless they wanted their head bitten off.

He paced. "I'm taking it hostilely if I have to."

"I see."

"I could use an escort."

Escort.

"I need someone I can count on. Most of all—" he crossed his arms and his enigmatic black gaze bored into hers "—I need someone willing to pretend to be my lover."

Lover.

Her hands went damp and she discreetly wiped them at her sides. "Lover." When his long steps brought him over to her, she instinctively backed away until her calves hit a small ottoman.

Unperturbed, Marcos headed over to the bookshelf, his strides sure and unhurried. "Would you be interested in doing this for me?"

Her head whizzed with unwelcome, naughty thoughts. Thoughts of Mexico and Marcos. Martinis and Marcos. Mariachis and Marcos. "Yes, definitely." But what exactly did he mean by *pretend?* "So what would you expect of me, for how long?" An unprecedented thrill was trickling along her veins.

He rummaged through the books, moving tome after tome. "A week as my escort in Monterrey, and perhaps some work after hours until I'm able to close. I'll be sure to handle your...little problem."

"That's all?"

He shot her a look of incredulity. "That's not enough?"

She just smiled. And waited.

And watched.

The muscles under his shirt flexed as he reached the top shelf and pulled out a huge leather volume.

"Maybe your company at the Fintech dinner?" he continued, winged eyebrows flying up. "Would you mind? Going with me?"

She fiddled with her pearls, unable to stop fidgeting. "You... I can always arrange a date for you."

His lips curved upward as he waved the heavy book in her line of vision as easily as if it were a mere piece of paper. "I don't want a date, Miss Hollis. Here. You can take this—a bit about Monterrey, if you'd like." He set it on the ottoman. He had a lovely, lazy kind of smile, and she felt it curl her toes.

"I feel like I'm robbing you blind," she said, lifting the shiny book.

He paused in the middle of the room and stared at her with his deep gypsy eyes. "If I allowed it, it wouldn't be robbery, would it."

She saw his cool, brief smile and flattened the book tight against her breasts when they pricked. Traitors. But he'd smiled three times tonight. Three. Or more? Three or more just had to be a record.

"You're an asset to my company," he continued in an unnaturally husky voice, stalking back around the desk. "A week of your time is valuable to me. You're hard-working, smart. Loyal. You've gained my trust, Virginia, and my admiration—both difficult feats."

A feathery sensation coursed along her skin. She was certain he used that same self-assured tone in his meetings, but she wondered if it had the same thrilling effect on the members of his board.

When she couldn't seem to find anything useful to do other than ogle stupidly, she automatically did what she always did to cure herself. She set the book aside and began arranging the papers at the edge of his desk—from a messy pile to a neat pile. "T-thank you for the compliments. I enjoy working at Fintech very much. And for you...of course. Which is why I don't want to jeopardize my position."

She continued arranging, aware that he was doing nothing—nothing—but towering a few feet away and watching her. Like he did in the office sometimes. He would stop what he was doing and watch with those black, exciting eyes.

"What will we say at the office?" she rambled.

Gossip could be ruthless at Fintech. To think Lindsay or Mrs. Fuller might believe she'd done something unprofessional to land a business trip with Marcos gripped her with unease.

When Marcos didn't reply, she looked up and caught the wicked sparkle in his eyes. She had the strangest sensation that he'd been staring at her bottom. "We will say that I ordered you to accompany me, of course. You are my assistant, after all."

His brows drew together and he peered at her hard, as though daring her to argue with him.

But a pang struck her right where it hurt; she knew she could never be more than an assistant to him. He was Marcos Allende. He could be Zeus himself, he was so unattainable.

Virginia was dreaming if she wanted more than a seat outside his office. Dreaming if she thought the desire in his eyes was for her. Dreaming to think that, even if it were, he'd do something about it and she'd dare let him.

No. She could not, would not allow herself to continue

harboring those foolish nightly fantasies about him. The daily ones had to go, too. It was hopeless, and it was hurtful, and it was stupid. He was offering her an assignment.

When the pile couldn't be a more perfect tower, she straightened it with as much dignity as she could muster. "I'd be happy to be your escort."

He nodded slowly. "Good. Great. Excellent." His voice was strangely terse, so utterly rich it seemed to sink into her body until it pulsed inside of her. "I knew we'd come to an agreement, then."

Dealing with a tumult of emotions without betraying herself proved difficult. Excitement warred with worry, gratitude with desire.

One week with him in Mexico. Playing his escort, his *lover*—a role Virginia had slipped into plenty of times in her mind. But this would be real, a real pretense, where she—inexperienced and naive in the ways of men—would pretend to be lover to a hunk, god and legend. Where she could even seize the moment, do something reckless she would no doubt come to regret and plant a kiss on the lips of the man who was unknowingly responsible for Virginia not wanting others. Did she dare? Did she fly? Did she have magic powers?

Was there even the possibility of being a good pretend lover to him after he'd dated actresses, duchesses, centerfolds?

Growing more and more unsettled at her new assignment, she picked up the book, *Monterrey: Tras el Tiempo,* and headed for the door, stealing one last glimpse of him. "Thank you, Marcos. For…everything. Good night."

"Virginia." When she was halfway down the hall, he caught up and seized her wrist, urging her around. His clasp sent a shiver skidding up her arm. "It's a five-hour flight. I mean to leave tomorrow afternoon. Can you be ready by then?"

Ready, she thought wildly.

She could be a virgin Mayan princess prepared her whole life for this ultimate sacrifice, be an Anne Boleyn laughingly led to her beheading, and she would *still* not be ready for Marcos Allende.

But she smiled. Her nod came out jerky.

He seized her chin and raised it slightly. She sucked in a breath at the contact, and the tips of her breasts brushed against his chest. "Will you be ready, Virginia?" he persisted.

Her legs quivered. All kinds of things moved inside her body. His breath was hot and fragrant on her face, and his lush, mobile mouth was so close, a moan rose to her throat, trapped there. Like the wanting of a year, trapped there.

How would he *feel* against her? His mouth? His hands?

He was so hard all over, so unlike any other man she'd known. He made her feel safe and protected and special, but he also made her burn, frightened her with the way she needed *something* from him more than she could possibly bear or understand.

She suppressed a shiver. "I'll be ready," she assured, a nervous excitement flourishing in her breast as she took a healthy step back. "Thank you. I know…I know you could ask someone else to do this for you. And I doubt you'd have to pay for her company."

His eyes smoldered, and his face went taut with some unnameable emotion. "Yes, but I want you."

I want you.

A ribbon of hope unfurled inside her. It feathered from the top of her head down to the soles of her feet. She didn't trust it. Marcos didn't mean the words the way they had sounded to her ears. Ears starved for anything he ever said to her.

She told herself, firmly, until it was embedded in her brain, that Marcos wanted someone trustworthy, someone biddable, and his lionlike instinct surely prodded him to help her.

And, oh, how she had wanted to be different. To him. Not

charity. Not like his stepbrother, a reckless playboy Marcos had to rescue time after time—not like all the strangers and friends who called him every day, seeking his counsel, his power, his help.

Everyone wanted something of Marcos Allende, for underneath the hard exterior lay a man with a strong, solid heart of gold. His faith in people was inspiring, his ruthlessness rivaled only by his mercy. Marcos…took care of you. And those early mornings when Virginia had stepped into his office to find his broad shoulders bent over the desk, his shirt rolled up to his elbows, his silky black hair falling over his forehead, his voice husky and his eyes tired from lack of sleep, her heart had ached with wanting to take care of that big, proud warrior. *Who gives you back what you give, Marcos Allende?*

Is there anyone out there who takes care of you for a change?

Now she determined that whatever he wanted, she would give. "You won't regret it, Marcos," she softly promised. "Helping me, I mean."

His lips twitched. That amused smile did things to her stomach, but it didn't seem to reach his eyes. Those remained hooded, unreadable. He ran the back of one finger down her cheek, the touch sparking fire. "It is I who hopes you never regret this visit."

Two

"Your new lover?"

Silent, Marcos stood at the living room window and broodingly watched the car pull away with Virginia inside it. From the penthouse, the Lincoln looked like a sleek black beetle, slipping into the intermittent traffic before the apartment building.

The pressure in his chest mounted with the distance.

His blood still pumped hot inside his veins and his head swam with a thousand thoughts, all of them X-rated.

"Or a mistress maybe?"

Twisting around, he faced his newest guest, the inquisitive Jack Williams—ex-corporate spy and now self-made millionaire. He was helping himself to a bag of nuts he'd obtained from the bar.

"My assistant," Marcos said tonelessly, swirling his newly poured Scotch in his hand. The cubes clinked in the glass.

Jack had arrived promptly at eleven as promised—the tall, blond Texan was never late, and, like a golden retriever listening to a particularly silent whistle, he had cocked his head when he spotted Virginia almost in Marcos's arms. As she whispered goodbye, Marcos's own instincts had flared to life and whispered that she wanted to stay.

But when "Williams the Bastard"—as the press had dubbed him—said he'd deliver, he delivered. And unfortunately what Marcos expected couldn't wait.

Still, he couldn't allow his friend to get the wrong impression of her, so he lifted his glass in a mocking toast. "She makes good coffee."

Jack popped an almond into his mouth and munched. "Aha. In bed?"

Marcos crossed the living room and headed back into the office, Jack trailing behind him.

Cranky, frustrated and exhausted, he set the glass atop a stack of papers on his desk and sank into the high-backed leather seat. "I'm not that man, Jack. Never mix business with pleasure, remember?"

But Virginia's sweet, fragrant scent lingered in the air. A torment to his straining body. A mockery to his words.

He respected his employees, took pride in being regarded as a man with moral fiber. And yet when it came to Virginia Hollis, it seemed he was reduced to the instincts of a caveman.

His friend's smooth, easy chuckle coming from the threshold somehow cranked up his frustration. "I remember. But the question is: do *you?* Should I have fetched a spoon, buddy? You looked ready to eat her."

Marcos would have scoffed. He certainly didn't welcome the canny twinkle in Jack's eye. But then he remembered the desperate urge he'd had to kiss Virginia…the exquisite scent of her skin, so close to his…the surprisingly fine feel of her in his arms, stirring and enticing beyond belief…

His chest cramped with emotion as he dragged a hand down his hot face. "Perhaps the old adage is true, and some rules are meant to be broken—especially if you're the moron living by them."

"Don't go there, Marcos." Jack pushed away from the door, dead serious. "I've been there. Not fun, man. Not fun for you, definitely not fun for her. Office affairs always end badly—no matter how well you plan them when you begin."

Marcos pondered the massive, crowded bookcase on the wall across from him. A near bursting sensation was lodged in the pit of his gut. He didn't want to hurt her. Hell, he hadn't wanted to *want* her.

Diablos, but he'd been sexually frustrated since the day he'd hired her. She was demure, desperate and determined, and Marcos had feared she'd be a distraction. But he hadn't counted on the fact that his primitive response to her would reach such a fever pitch.

"I've never gotten involved with an employee in my life— but she's different, Jack. And yes, I am aware of how that sounds."

Reclining in his seat with a grimace, he opened his cuff buttons and rolled up his sleeves.

He was actually considering, perhaps he was even past considering and had already made up his mind, giving them both what they'd wanted for months.

He was a man, flesh and blood like all the others. There was only so much he could stand. And Virginia…no matter how energetically she tried to conceal her reactions to him, she responded. Viscerally, primitively—a woman underneath the tidy assistant after all. A sweet, lovely woman who knew instinctively when a man wanted her. No, not wanted— Marcos *burned* for her.

And now he'd asked—practically demanded—she spend a week with him. Pretending to be his lover. At a time when all his energies, all his attention, needed to be on the one prize he'd sought to gain for so long.

Allende.

He hadn't been certain whether to ask her as escort. She was too much a temptation to play lovers with, and in order to successfully achieve his goals, focus was key.

But tonight the lovely Virginia—alone and financially abandoned by her family, something Marcos could identify with—had turned to him for help.

Tonight, as he'd gazed into her bright, fierce eyes, he couldn't deny himself any longer.

He wanted her.

He'd offered her a position for a week, true, but that was merely a guise for what he really wanted to do.

Her powerful effect would linger with him long after he left his office at night. He thought of her continually, every hour. He relived their encounters in his mind sometimes, enjoyed hearing her laugh at Lindsay's antics when his office doors were parted. He could not push her image away at night and loathed to see her in trouble when she seemed to seek so little of it for herself.

He'd made a mental list long ago with plenty of valid reasons to leave her alone.

She was an innocent, he was not. She was vulnerable, he could hurt her. She was his employee, he was her boss. There were dozens of reasons to stay the hell away from Virginia.

The ways she'd looked at him tonight pulverized them all.

"Here. I have just the thing to cheer you up." Jack stepped outside and returned rummaging through his leather briefcase. He yanked out a manila folder and held it out. "There you go, big man. Your wish is my command."

Marcos plucked the file from his hand and immediately honed in on the name printed across the tab. Marissa Galvez.

He smiled darkly. "Ah, my rainmaker. Everything here, I assume?"

"Everything on Marissa and her sleazy little deals. She's quite a busy little bee. You'll find it to be riveting reading. Took me a while, as you can see—but I did give you my word to have it ready by tonight."

Marcos skimmed through the pages, not surprised that the file was as thick as the woman was scheming.

Marissa Galvez. A shaft of anger sliced through him. The lady had hopes of a reconciliation before discussing numbers?

Of course she did. She read *Forbes*. Was smart enough to realize the son was worth more than the father she'd left him for, not thousands or millions, but billions. She knew the company, which should have rightfully been *his,* was prime for takeover and it wouldn't take much but a few savvy connections to learn it had been Marcos who'd been buying the outstanding stock.

Unfortunately, insulting Marissa's renewed interest in him wouldn't do to accomplish his goals. But a beautiful, smiling lover would slowly and surely take care of her dreams of reconciliation—and let them get down to the real business at hand.

Allende. *My company.*

"Mind telling me how you're going to convince the delectable woman to sell? Without succumbing to her request for some personal attention before discussing numbers?" Jack queried.

Marcos lunged to his feet, waving the evidence in the Texan's face. "With this. It's my game now, my rules." He met his friend's sharp, blue-eyed stare and his lips flattened to a grim, strained line. "Allende is in a vulnerable position. Sooner or later, she'll have to sell."

"Not to you, she doesn't."

Marcos shrugged disinterestedly. "She knows she's game for a hostile takeover. And she knows I'm the shark after her.

She wouldn't have called if she didn't want to get on my good side."

And I've got my pretty, green-eyed "lover."

"Will she?"

And her pretty little mouth. "What?"

"Get on your good side?"

"When you start wearing a tutu, Jack. Of course not."

Distaste filled him as he recalled her phone call. Dangling Allende up to him like bait, proposing they discuss it in her bed. She'd played with him as a naive, noble, seventeen-year-old boy, but it would be an ice age in hell before she played with the man.

"She called because she wants you back," Jack pointed out.

"Fortunately, I have an escort," he said and headed to the window, a part of him somehow expecting to see the Lincoln. "Being I will be conveniently taken, we'll have to forego the personal and get down to the numbers."

"I see now. So the lovely lady is key."

Those eyes. Big, bright, clear green, and so expressive he thought she'd pummeled his gut when she'd looked at him so adoringly. She made him feel…noble. Decent. Desperate to save her ten times over in exchange for another worshipful gaze.

When she'd called to request a moment of his time only hours ago, he'd allowed himself a brief flight of fantasy. He fantasized she'd been ready to succumb to him, ready to admit what already threatened to become inevitable. Even as he allowed himself the luxury of the fantasy, he knew she was too cautious and respectable for that.

It was up to him now. What was he going to do?

He shot Jack a sidelong look. "Marissa will get what's coming to her." And Virginia…

Jack swept up his briefcase with flair. "The devil on a Falcon jet, yes." He saluted from the threshold and flashed his signature I'm-Jack-the-Ripper grin. "I'll let you pack, my friend."

"My gratitude to you, Williams. And send the bill to Mrs. Fuller this week, she'll take care of it."

When Jack said an easy "will do" and disappeared, Marcos swallowed the last of his Scotch, his eyebrows furrowing together as he thought of the demure strand of pearls around Virginia's neck tonight. His woman wouldn't wear such little pearls. She'd wear diamonds. Tahitians. Emeralds.

With a swell of possessiveness, he brought to mind the lean, toned form of her body, watched countless times across his office desk, countless times when it had been by sheer determination that he'd forced his scrutiny back to his work.

A size six, he predicted, and promptly pulled his contact list from the top drawer and flipped through the pages.

If she was playing his lover, then one thing was certain: Virginia Hollis would look the part.

In the quiet interior of the Fixed Base Operator which specialized in servicing company jets, Marcos stood with his hands in his pockets. He brimmed with anticipation and gazed out the window from the spacious sitting area while the Falcon 7X jet—a sleek, white dove and one of his faster babies—got fueled.

He'd like to blame his simmering impatience on the deal he was about to negotiate. But the truth was, his assistant was late, and he was impatient to see *her*.

Now a door of opportunity was wide open for them. An opportunity to interact outside the busy, hectic pace of his office. An opportunity to step out of their roles and, if they chose to, temporarily into a new one.

She'll pretend to be my lover.

That she had accepted to aid him in this manner made

him feel heady. For how long would they be able to pretend and only pretend? Three days, three hours, three minutes?

In the back of the room, the glass doors rolled open. The sounds of traffic sailed into the building and Marcos swung around. To watch Virginia stroll inside.

A balloon of protectiveness blossomed in his chest.

The only thing untidy about his assistant today was her hair. Wild, windblown and uncontrollable. The ebony curls framed a lovely oval face and eyes that were green and clear and thick-lashed. Hauling a small black suitcase behind her, she paused to store a bag of peanuts in the outside zippered compartment. The mint-green V-neck sweater she wore dipped sexily to show the barest hint of cleavage. His mouth went dry.

She straightened that agile body of hers and swiped a wave of ebony curls behind her shoulder. The scent of citrus—lemons, oranges, everything that made him salivate—wafted through the air as she continued hauling her suitcase forward. Christ, she was a sexpot.

"Virginia," he said.

Her head swiveled to his. "Marcos."

He smiled. The sight of her face, warm in the sunlight, made his lungs constrict. She wore no makeup except for a gloss, and with her curls completely free, she was the most enchanting thing he'd ever seen.

Licking her lips as he came forward, she pulled the suitcase up and planted it at her feet—a barrier between their bodies. "You got a head start on me," she said. She spoke in a throaty, shaky voice that revealed her nervousness.

He eyed her lips. Burnished a silky pink today, inciting him to taste.

"I apologize, I had some last-minute work out of the office."

Dragging in a breath, he jerked his chin in the direction of the long table down the hall, offering coffee, cookies, napkins—all that Virginia liked to toil with. "Fix yourself coffee if you want. We'll board in a few minutes."

"You? Coffee?"

Somberly he shook his head, unable to prevent noticing the subtle sway of her skirt-clad hips as she left her compact black suitcase with him and walked away.

He was fascinated. By the sweet-smelling, sexy package of Virginia Hollis. Five feet four inches of reality. Of *pretend* lover.

Cursing under his breath, he snatched her suitcase handle and rolled the bag up to his spot by the window. The pilots were storing his luggage, consisting mostly of shopping bags from Neiman Marcus.

He crossed his arms as he waited for their signal. The file the infallible Jack Williams had given him last night provided him with more than enough ammo to persuade Marissa to sell, yet even the knowledge of emerging victorious didn't make this particular task any easier. You could crush a bug in your fist and it still didn't mean you would enjoy it. But Allende—a transport company on its last breath, flailing for help—had his name on it.

It was his. To resuscitate or to murder.

Virginia drew up beside him and he went rigid, inhumanly aware of her body close to his. She was a subtle, scented, stirring presence.

Without so much as moving his head, he let his eyes venture to the front of her sweater. The fabric clung to the small, shapely, seductive swells of her breasts. A wealth of tenderness flooded him. Virginia had come dressed as his assistant in the sweater, her typical knee-length gray skirt, the simple closed-toe shoes with no personality. "I'm afraid this won't do," he murmured.

A smile danced on her lips as she tipped her face up in bewilderment. She seemed animated today, no more the worried siren begging for his assistance last night. "What won't do?"

Virginia. With her perfect oval face, creamy, elegant throat and bow-shaped morsel of a mouth that invited him to nibble. It really seemed easier to stop breathing than to continue saying *no* to those marshmallow-soft lips. "The sweater," he said quietly, signaling the length of her body with his hand. "The skirt. The sensible shoes. It won't do, Miss Hollis."

She set her coffee cup and napkin on a side table, then tucked her hair behind her ear. "I did pack a few dresses."

"Did you." His eyebrows furrowed together as he surveyed her pearls. "Designer dresses?"

"Why, no."

He raised his hand to the pearl necklace. "How attached are you," he whispered, trailing his finger across the glossy bumps, "to wearing these?"

She watched him for a moment, a telling wariness in her voice. "They were Mother's."

"Pretty. Very pretty." The pent-up desire that blazed inside him textured his voice. "You see, my lover…might wear something else." He was playing with fire. He didn't care. "My woman—" he plucked a pearl between two fingers "—would wear Tahitians. Diamonds. Emeralds."

Her eyes danced. "Are you afraid I won't look presentable?"

He dropped his hands and shot her a dead-serious look. "I'm afraid you will look too much like my assistant and not my lover."

But she kept on smiling, kept on enchanting him. "I see."

He frowned now. "Understand me, Virginia. If I'd wanted to be seen with my assistant, I'd have brought Mrs. Fuller."

This made her gasp, and the gasp did not make his scowl vanish. He nodded towards the Falcon. "Your new wardrobe is in the plane. There's a room in the back. Change."

Three

Of all the highhandedness, of all the *arrogance,* of all the bosses in the world—she had to be in debt to *Marcos.* Undoubtedly the most complicated.

While the jet motors hummed in the background, Virginia slipped into the slinky patterned dress inside the windowless little room at the back of the plane. Damn him. She had agreed to his request, but how was she supposed to reply to his autocratic commands? Worse, the clothes were divine. She couldn't in her right mind stay annoyed at a man with such exquisite taste. Her knight in shining armor.

Enthralled by how slight and satiny the dress felt against her body, she ran three fingers down the length of her hips, wishing there was a mirror to let her visually appreciate the dress's exquisite, plunging back. *And how is this necessary to his plan?* she wondered.

Gathering her courage with a steady intake of breath, she forced herself to step outside.

Throughout the tasteful wood and leather interior, the air

crackled with the suppressed energy of his presence. His
head was bent. His powerful, well-built body overwhelmed
a cream-colored, plush leather seat, and his hair—abused by
his hands during the flight—gleamed in the sunlight as he
read through a massive leather tome. He was clad all in black,
and the short-sleeved polo shirt he wore revealed tanned,
strong forearms corded with veins. Watching him, big and
proud and silent, completely engrossed and unaware of her
gaze, she felt like sighing.

With a quick mental shake, she walked down the wide
plane aisle, noting the screen embedded in the wood-paneled
wall behind Marcos's seat. The electronic map showed
the plane just three red dashes away from the little dot of
Monterrey. At least one more hour.

As she eased in between their seats, intent on taking her
place across from him, one huge hand shot out and manacled
her wrist. She was spun around, and she gasped. Then there
was nothing to pry those glimmering eyes away from her, no
shield from the scorching possessiveness flickering in their
depths.

"No," he rasped, his voice hoarsened by how little he'd
spoken during the flight.

A melting sensation spread down her thighs, his accent
too delicious to not enjoy. *No, don't sit yet,* she thought he
meant, but she couldn't be sure. No one could ever be too sure
of anything with Marcos. Maybe it was *no* to the dress!

Aware of her chest heaving too close to his face, she tried
to pry her wrist free but failed miserably. "I changed. Wasn't
that what you wanted?"

He cocked his head farther back and stared, his grip
loosening slightly. "You're angry at me." •

"I…" She jerked her chin toward the book on his lap,
wanting, needing him to remove his hand. "Please. Read."

For a woman who'd strived to become invisible for years,
the last thing she felt now was unseen. The filmy Issa London

dress hugged her curves subtly, the wrap-around style tied with a bow at her left hip. The fabric felt so feminine she became utterly conscious of her body—and how he peered at it in interest.

"You approve of the clothes I bought you, *amor?*" he said huskily.

Amor? A jolt went through her at the endearment. Panicking, she tugged with more force and whispered, halfheartedly, "You can let go of me now."

His gaze pierced her, his unyielding hand burning her wrist. By the way his touch spread like a wildfire, her boss may as well have been touching her elsewhere. Where her breasts ached, where the back of her knees tingled, where her nerves sparkled and where she felt hot and painfully aware of being empty.

He released her. So abruptly she almost stumbled.

Still reeling, Virginia sank into her seat like a deflated balloon. Her pulse thundered. Her hands shook as she strapped on her seat belt.

His intense regard from across the aisle became a living, breathing thing. "Does a man's interest offend you?" he asked silkily.

Blushing furiously, she propped her purse on her lap. "Did you know Monterrey has over five million people now?" She shoved the maps she'd printed at the office and lists of Spanish words back in her purse.

He slapped the book shut and let it drop with a resounding thump at his feet. "Would *my* interest offend you, Virginia?"

She squinted at him, expecting a laugh, a chuckle, a smile at least.

He was perfectly sober. Excruciatingly handsome and sober.

Oh, no. No, no, no, he wouldn't do this. She was prepared

to do a job, but she was not prepared to allow herself to become a man's…plaything.

No matter how much she fantasized about him in private.

With a nervous smile, Virginia shook a chastising finger at him, but it trembled. "Mr. Allende, the closer we've gotten to Mexico, the stranger you've become."

Silence.

For an awful second, her blatant claim—part teasing and part not—hung suspended in the air. Virginia belatedly bit her lip. What had possessed her to say that to her boss? She curled her accusing finger back into her hand, lowering it in shame.

Sitting in a deceptively relaxed pose, he crossed his arms over his broad chest and regarded her with an unreadable expression. Then he spoke in that hushed, persuasive way of his, "Do you plan to call me *Mr. Allende* when you're out there pretending to be my lover?"

Self-conscious and silently berating herself, Virginia tucked the skirt of her dress under her thighs, her hands burrowing under her knees. "I didn't mean to insult you."

"I'm not insulted."

She racked her brain for what to say. "I don't know what came over me."

He leaned forward with such control that even a glare might have been more welcome by her. "You call me Marcos most of the time. You call me Marcos when you want my favors. Why now, today, do you call me Mr. Allende?"

She looked away, feeling as if her heart were being wrung. He spoke so quietly, almost pleadingly, that he could be saying something else to her—something that did not smack her with misery.

Because I've never been alone with you for so long, she thought.

She hauled in a ragged breath and remained silent.

The plane tilted slightly, eventually coming in for a landing as smoothly as it had flown. Its speed began to ease. If only her hammering heart would follow.

They taxied down a lane decorated with large open plane hangars, and she fixed her attention on the screen behind him, resolved to smooth out the awkwardness. "Do you believe Allende will be a safe investment for Fintech?" she asked. She knew it was all that remained of his past. His mother had passed away long before his father had.

"It's poorly managed." He extracted his BlackBerry from his trouser pocket and powered it on. "Transport vehicles have been seized by the cartels. Travel is less safe these days in this country. For it to become successful, strict security measures will need to be put in place, new routes, new personnel, and this will mean money. So, no. It isn't a safe investment."

She smiled in admiration as he swiftly skimmed through his text messages. He oozed strength. Strength of mind, of body, of purpose. "You'll make it gold again," she said meaningfully, still not believing that, God, she'd called him *strange* to his face!

He lifted his head. "I'm tearing it apart, Virginia."

The plane lurched to a stop. The engines shut down. The aisle lit up with a string of floor lights.

Virginia was paralyzed in her seat, stunned. "You plan to destroy your father's business," she said in utter horror, a sudden understanding of his morose mood barreling into her.

His hard, aquiline face unreadable, he thrust his phone into his pocket and silently contemplated her. "It's not *his* anymore." His face was impassive, but his eyes probed into her. "It was meant to be mine when he passed away. I built it with him."

This morning, between phone calls, coffee, copies and errands, she'd gotten acquainted with Monterrey from afar. Learned it was a valley surrounded by mountains. Industrial, cosmopolitan, home of the wealthy and, at the very outskirts of the city, home of the poor. Indisputably the most prominent part of northern Mexico. Conveniently situated for Allende Transport, of course, as a means to import, export and travel—but also conveniently situated for those who imported and exported illegal substances. Like the cartels.

Allende wasn't a bouquet of roses, she supposed, but she'd never expected Marcos willingly to attempt to destroy it.

"You look as if I'd confessed to something worse," he noted, not too pleased himself.

"No. It's only that—" She checked herself before continuing this time. "That's not like you. To give up on something. You've never given up on Santos no matter what he does."

His intense expression lightened considerably. "My brother is a person—Allende is not."

Mightily aware of how out of character this decision was, Virginia ached to remind him he'd dedicated his life to helping companies in crisis, had taken under his wing businesses and even people no one else had faith in but Marcos, but instead she rose to her feet. Unfolding like a long, sleek feline just awakened to the hunt, Marcos followed her up. And up.

"Virginia, this isn't Chicago." He loomed over her by at least a head. His face was impassive, but his eyes probed into her. "If you want to sightsee, you'll be accompanied by me. Too dangerous to be alone here."

Dangerous.

The word caused gooseflesh on her skin.

Remembering her research on the city, she peered out a window as two uniformed *aduanales* and twice as many armed *militares* marched up to the plane. She'd heard military men customarily accompanied the Mexican customs agents but she was still floored by the intimidating sight. The copilot unlatched the door up front and descended to meet them.

She couldn't see much of the city at this late hour, but what she'd read online had mesmerized her. She would have even thought the setting romantic if his careful warning weren't dawning on her. "Dangerous," she said. "What must it be like for the people who live here?"

"Difficult." He rammed his book into a leather briefcase and zipped it shut. "Kidnapping rate has risen alarmingly during the last couple of years. Mothers are lifted outside the supermarkets, kids out of their schools, members of both government and police are bribed to play blind man to what goes on."

A rope of fear stretched taut around her stomach. "That's so sad."

She took one last look out the plane window. Nothing moved but the Mexican flag flapping by the customs building.

"It looks so calm," she protested.

"Under the surface nothing is calm." As he stood there, over six feet of virile overpowering man, he looked just a tad tired, and human, and so much sexier than behind his massive desk. He looked touchable. *Touchable.*

Under the surface nothing is calm. Not even me.

"Mrs. Fuller said you grew up here," she remarked as she eyed the fruit assortment on a table near the front of the plane.

"From when I was eight to eighteen," he answered. He stared, mildly puzzled, as she grabbed two green apples and slipped them into her purse.

"In case we get hungry," she explained sheepishly.

His eyes glittered with humor. "If you get hungry, you tell me and I'll make certain you're fed."

"What made you leave the city?" Leave a place that was beautiful and deadly. A place that gave out the message: Don't trust. You're not safe. And the one that had built a man like Marcos Allende, with an impenetrable core.

He braced one arm on the top wood compartment, waiting for the pilots to give them leave to descend. "Nothing here for me. Nothing in España either."

She loved the way he pronounced that. España. The way his arm stretched upward, long and sinewy, rippling under his black shirt before he let it drop. Somber, he gazed into her eyes, and the concern she saw in his gave her flutters. "Are you tired?"

"I'm fine." *You're here,* she thought.

The look that came to his eyes. The way he appraised her.

Virginia could've sworn there could be no flaw in her entire body. Nothing in this world more perfect to those dark, melted-chocolate eyes than she was.

His eyes fell to her lips and lingered there for an electric moment.

"Virginia." He closed the space between them. One step. All the difference between breathing or not. All the difference between being in control of your senses and being thrust into a twister.

He leaned over as he pried her purse from her cramped hands. His fingers brushed the backs of hers and a sizzle shot up her arm.

"Why are you nervous?" The low, husky whisper in her ear made her stomach tumble. She felt seared by his nearness, branded, as though he were purposely making her aware that his limits extended to breaching hers. She felt utterly... claimed. "You've fidgeted all day."

So he had been aware of her?

Like...a predator. Watching from afar. Planning, plotting, savoring the prey.

Why was this exciting?

His breath misted across the tender skin behind her ear. "Because of me?"

Her muscles gelled. *Because I want you.*

She took a shaky step back, singed to the marrow of her bones but smiling as though she was not. "I always get a charge after being rescued."

"Ahh." He drew out the sound, infusing it with a wealth of meaning. "So do I. After…rescuing." He swung his arm back so her purse dangled from one hooked finger behind his shoulder.

When the pilot announced they were clear, he signaled with an outstretched arm toward the plane steps. "Ladies first."

She warily stepped around his broad, muscled figure. "I admit I'm not used to your silences still."

His gaze never strayed from hers as she went around. "So talk next time," he said. "To me."

Right. Next time. Like he inspired one to make intimate revelations. And like he'd have another company to take over with the help of a "lover."

As both pilots conversed with the customs officials, Virginia stopped a few feet from the gaping doorway. Warmth from outside stole into the air-conditioned cabin, warming her cool skin. But she found she couldn't descend just yet.

She'd do anything to get her father out of his mess, yet suddenly felt woefully unprepared to play anyone's lover. Especially Marcos's lover. No matter how much she ached for the part and planned to get it right.

She pivoted on her heels to find him standing shockingly close. She craned her neck to meet his gaze. "Marcos, I'm going to need you to…tell me. What to do."

He wore an odd expression on his face, part confusion and part amusement. The smile he slowly delivered made her flesh pebble. "You may step out of the plane, Miss Hollis."

Laughing, she gave an emphatic shake of her head. "I mean, regarding my role. I will need to know what you suggest that I do. I'm determined, of course, but I'm hoping to get some pointers. From you."

His lids dropped halfway across his eyes. He lifted a loose fist and brushed his knuckles gently down her cheek. The touch reached into the depths of her soul. "Pretend you want me."

A tremor rushed down her limbs. Oh, God, he was so sexy. She was torn between latching on to his tempting, unyielding lips and running for her life. "I will, of course I will," she breathed.

A cloak of stillness came over her—so that all that moved, all she was aware of, was his hand. As he trailed his thumb down to graze her shoulder and in a ghost of a touch swept a strand of hair back, he swallowed audibly. "Look at me like you always do."

"How?"

"You know how." There was so much need in his eyes, a thirst she didn't know how to appease, which called to a growing, throbbing, aching void inside of her. "Like you care for me, like you need me."

"I do." She shook her cluttered head, straightening her thoughts. "I mean, I am. I *will*."

She shut her eyes tight, fearing he would see the truth in them. Fearing Marcos would realize she'd been secretly enamored of him all along. Since the very first morning she'd stepped into his office, she had wanted to die—the man was so out of this world. So male. So dark.

And now…what humiliation for him to discover that, if he crooked his finger at her, Virginia would go to him.

He chuckled softly—the sound throaty, arrogant, male. "Good."

His large hand gripped her waist and urged her around to face the open plane door a few feet away. She went rigid at the shocking contact. Longing flourished. Longing for more, for that hand, but on her skin and not her clothes, sliding up or down, God, doing anything.

Dare she dream? Dare she let herself long just a little,

without feeling the remorse she always did? Like she could indulge in a healthy fantasy now and then?

She wiggled free, sure of one thing: dissolving into a puddle of want was not what she should be doing just now.

"But…what do you want me to do, exactly?" she insisted, carefully backing up one step as she faced him. His eyebrows met in a scowl. He didn't seem to like her retreating. "This is important to you, right?" she continued.

"Señor Allende, pueden bajar por favor?"

Spurred to action by the voices on the platform, Virginia descended the steps. Marcos quickly took his place beside her.

They followed two uniformed officials toward a rustic, one-story building rivaled in size by Marcos's jet. A small control tower, which looked abandoned at this hour, stood discreetly to the building's right. A gust of hot, dry wind picked up around them, bouncing on the concrete and lifting the tips of her hair.

Virginia grabbed the whirling mass with one hand and pinned it with one fist at her nape. Marcos held the glass doors open for her. "No need to pretend just now, Miss Hollis," he said. "We can do that later."

His eyes glimmered dangerously with something. Something frightening. A promise. A request.

Her heart flew like the wind inside her, bouncing between her ribs, almost lifting the tips of her feet from the ground. Warily she passed through the bridge of his arm, one word's haunting echo resounding in her mind. And for the dread that began to take hold, it might have been a death sentence.

Later.

Fifteen minutes later, after a brisk *"Bienvenidos a Mexico"* from the *aduanales*, they were settled in the back of a silver Mercedes Benz, their luggage safely tucked in the trunk.

"A Garza Garcia, si?" the uniformed driver asked as he eased behind the wheel.

"Por favor," Marcos said.

His palm tingled. The one he'd touched her with. The one that had reached out to cup the lovely curve of her waist and caused Virginia to back away. From his touch.

Frowning, he checked his watch—it was ten past midnight. Wanting had *never* been like this. You wanted a watch, or a house, or money, but wanting this particular woman was no such whim. It was a need, something pent-up for too long, something so valued you were hesitant to have, or break, or tarnish, or hurt.

The car swerved onto the deserted highway and Virginia tipped her face to the window, lightly tugging at the pearls around her neck.

"You had a decent trip, Señor Allende?" their driver asked.

"Yes," he said, stretching out his legs as far as he could without bumping his knee into the front seat.

Miles away, the distant core of the city of Monterrey glowed with lights. The sky was clear and veiled with gray, its shadow broken by a steady stream of streetlights rolling by.

"It's lovely here." Virginia transferred her purse to the nook at her feet then tapped a finger to the window. "Look at the mountains."

Her skin appeared luminous upon every brisk caress of the streetlights, and in the shadows her eyes glittered uncommonly bright. They sparkled with excitement.

He felt a tug at his chest. "I'll show you around tomorrow in daylight," he said curtly.

Her eyes slid over to his, grateful, alive eyes. "Thank you."

A heroic feeling feathered up his chest, and he pushed it aside.

During a lengthy quiet spell, the driver flicked on the radio and soft music filled the interior of the car. Virginia remained way over on the other end of the seat.

Not near enough...

He studied her figure, becoming fixated on the rounded breasts swelling under her clingy dress, the curve of her thigh and hip and small waist. Swirly black bits of hair tickled her shoulders. Her long, shapely legs had a satin shine to them, inviting him to wrap them around his body and spill days and weeks and months of wanting inside her.

He whispered, in a low murmur that excluded the driver, "Are you afraid of me?"

She stiffened. Pale, jade-green eyes rose to his for a second before her lashes dropped. "No. Why would you ask?"

Her shyness brought out the hunter in him, and it took effort on his part to keep under control. Go slowly with her... His heart began to pound. He patted his side. "You could come a little closer."

Ducking her head to hide a blush, she smoothed her hands along the front of her dress. Then she flicked a tiny knot of fabric from it. "Just haven't traveled in ages."

"You cringe at anyone's touch, or merely mine?"

She blinked. "Cringe? I'd never cringe if you...touched me."

The words *touched me* hovered between them like a dark, unleashed secret, an invitation to sin, and when Marcos at last responded to that, the thick lust in his voice was unmistakable. "You moved away when I urged you out of the plane. And when I helped you into the car."

"I was surprised." Her throat worked as she swallowed. Her eyes held his in the darkness. "I told you to tell me what to do."

She was whispering, so he whispered back.

"And I asked you to come closer just now."

A tense moment passed.

In silence, Marcos once again patted his side, this time more meaningfully.

After a moment's debate, Virginia seemed to quickly make up her mind. Thrusting out her chin at a haughty angle, she began to edge toward him. "If you're thinking I'm not good at this, I'll have you know I can pretend just fine."

Her scent stormed into his lungs. His nostrils twitched. His heart kicked. His temperature spiked.

Cautiously, as though petting a lion, she turned his hand over and set her cool, small palm on his. She gingerly laced her fingers through his. Lust kicked him in the groin at the unexpected touch. His head fell onto the back of the seat, a groan welling up in the back of his throat. Crucified by arousal, he dragged in a terse, uneven breath, squeezing his eyes shut.

She inched a little closer, tightening her grip. Her lips came to within a breath of his ear. "Does that satisfy you, Your Highness?"

He didn't let it show, the emotion that swept through him, but it made his limbs tremble. He said, thickly, "Come closer."

He wanted to jump her. He wanted all of her, right here, right now.

He inhaled deeply, his chest near bursting with the aroma of her. Clean, womanly, sweet. "Closer," he said, hearing the growl in his own words.

When she didn't, he glanced down at their joined hands. Hers was tiny and fair, nearly engulfed by his larger one. He ran the pad of his thumb along the back of hers, up the ridge of her knuckle, down the tiny smooth slope. She felt so good. And he felt eighteen again. "Soft," came his trancelike murmur.

Transfixed, she watched the movement of his thumb, her breasts stretching the material covering them as she inhaled. He dipped his head and discreetly rubbed his nose across the shiny, springy curls of her hair. Christ. Edible. All of her. He could smell her shampoo, wanted to plunge all ten fingers into her hair, turn her face up and kiss her lips. Softly, so he could savor her breath, go searching deep into her mouth.

Ducking his head so the driver wouldn't hear him, he whispered, "You might try to appear to enjoy my touch."

Their bodies created a heat, a dark intimate cocoon in the confined car interior, enhanced by the warmth of their whispers. "Marcos…"

His hand turned, capturing hers as she attempted to retrieve it. "Virginia."

Their gazes held. Like they did across his office, over the tops of people's heads, in the elevators. Those clear, infinite eyes always sought out his. To find him looking right back. Their fingers brushed at the pass of a coffee mug, a file, the phone. At contact their bodies seemed to flare up like matches—tense, coil, heat up the room. Even with a wall separating them, his awareness of her had escalated to alarming levels. And she'd been more fidgety with him than she had in months.

"We're pretending, remember?" he said, a husky reminder.

Pretend. The only way Marcos could think of that wouldn't involve her feelings, or his. The only way they might be able to—hell, what was this? It had been going on so long it felt like surrender—without anyone hurting in the end. Without their lives changing, breaking or veering off in separate ways because of it.

"Yes, I know."

"Then relax for me." Lightly securing her fingers between his, he delved his thumb into the center of her palm with a deep, intense stroke, aware of her audible intake of breath as he caressed. "Very good," he cooed. "I'm convinced you want me."

"Yes." Her voice was but a whisper, hinting at how the

sinuous, stroking circles of his thumb affected her. "I mean…
I'm trying to…appear that I do."

But she seemed as uncertain and startled as a mouse who
didn't know where to run to, and Marcos was very much
taking to the cat's role. He wanted to play, to corner, to
taste.

He glanced up. "Don't tax yourself too much, hmm."

Her warm, fragile fingers trembled in his. The excitement
of a new country had left her eyes, replaced by a wild, stormy
yearning. "I'm trying not to…get bored."

His thumb went deep at the center then eased back. "Hmm.
Yes. I can see you're fighting a yawn." His eyes ventured up
along the top of her head, taking in its gloss. "You have pretty
hair. Can I touch it?"

He did. It felt soft and silky under his fingers, tempting
him to dig in deeper, down to her scalp.

She made a sound in her throat, like a moan. A hunger
of the worst, most painful kind clawed inside him. She had
a way of staring at him with those big eyes like he was
something out of this world. It was a miracle he'd resisted
her this long.

"A man," he gruffly began, massaging the back of her
head as he greedily surveyed her features, "would be lucky
to make you his."

Her eyes sealed shut so tightly she seemed to be in
pain. She squirmed a little on the seat and, unbelievably,
came nearer. "You don't have to convince me. I'm already
pretending."

Her breasts brushed his rib cage, and the heat of her supple
body singed his flesh through their clothes. He intensified
the strokes of his fingers. "A man would be lucky to make
you his, Virginia," he repeated.

Her lashes fluttered upward, revealing her eyes. Pale
green, ethereal. Distrustful. "What are you doing?"

His gut tightened. *What does it look like I'm doing?* He

wanted to yank her onto his lap, feel his way up her little skirt, and kiss her mouth until her lips turned bright red. Her face blurred with his vision. With his need. He had to force himself to leave her hair alone.

She exhaled a string of broken air, then relaxed somewhat, shifting sideways on the leather seat. Facing him. Her smile faded. "Who are we fooling, Marcos, with this charade?"

"Marissa Galvez, Allende Transport's owner."

And maybe you. Definitely me.

He retrieved her hand from where it had gone to wring the hem of her dress and secured her wrist in his grip as he raised it. He turned it over and set a soft, lingering kiss at the center of her palm. A tiny, breathless gasp came from her.

"We must practice," he murmured, gazing into those deep, bottomless eyes.

"Oh." She shivered. Not moving away, and not moving closer, she allowed him to drag his lips along her open palm. She watched him through her lashes, her lips shuddering on each uneven breath.

"And why must we fool her?" Her question was a silky wisp.

"Because she wants me," he huskily answered. She tasted divine. Her skin was smooth and satiny under his lips, and he predicted every inch of her body would feel just like it. Perfect. "It wouldn't do to insult her." Against his mouth and lips, he felt the vibrant tremor that danced up her arm. Emboldened by her response, thirsting for more, he opened his mouth and gently grazed his teeth at the heel of her palm. "I happen to want someone else."

"I'm sure—" she began, swallowing audibly. "I'm sure you can have anyone you want."

"If I want her bad enough and put myself to task, yes." His lips closed and opened against her hand. Before he could restrain himself, he gave a lick at her palm. Pleasure pummeled through him. "And I've grown to want her...bad," he strained out, swallowing back a growl.

"Oh, that was..." Her hand wiggled as she tried prying it free. "I don't think..."

"Shh."

He held her wrist in a gentle grip and raised his head. He watched her expression soften, melt, as he whisked the pad of his thumb across her dampened palm, getting it wet. He lifted the glistening pad of his thumb to her lips, his timbre coated with arousal. "Pretend you like it when I do this."

A sound welled in the back of her throat as he stroked. She nodded wildly, her lips gleaming at each pass of his thumb. "Yes, yes, I'm pretending," she breathed.

He'd never seen a more erotic sight, felt a more erotic sensation, than playing with Virginia Hollis's quivering pink lips in the back of a moving car. "Umm. Me, too. I will pretend...you're her."

"Aha."

"And I very much want her." God, he enjoyed her unease, enjoyed seeing her pupils dilate, her breath shallow out.

"O-okay."

His thumb continued glancing, whisking, rubbing, right where his mouth wanted to be. He bent to whisper, to conspire together, just him and her. "Let's pretend...we're lovers, Virginia." His voice broke with the force of his desire, came out rough with wanting. "Pretend every night we touch each other...and kiss...and our bodies rock together. And when we find release—"

"Stop!" She pushed herself back with surprising force, sucking great gulps of air. "God, stop. Enough. Enough pretending tonight."

He tugged her closer. They were breathing hard and loud.

"You should kiss me," he said gruffly.

"Kiss you." She absently fingered his cross where it

peeked through the top opening of his shirt. He went utterly still—the gesture too sweet, too unexpected, too painful.

Her fingers reached his throat, then traced the links of the thick chain.

Too aware of this now, he dropped her hair and squeezed her elbow meaningfully. "Virginia. Your mouth. On mine."

They'd had foreplay for a year—with every glance, every flick of her hair, every smile.

She drew back and laughed, a choked, strained sound. "Now?" She couldn't seem to believe her eyes and ears, seemed stumped for words to deny him.

The car halted at a stoplight. A few cars drove up beside them. Marcos went still, glancing at her quietly until their car continued.

He had never wanted to feel a body as much as he wanted to feel hers.

And her mouth—he'd give anything to taste that mouth, was being for the first time in his life reckless, selfish, for that very mouth. A mouth that promised all the innocence he'd never had, trust, beauty, affection he'd never had.

Without any further thought, he pulled her close. "One kiss. Right now."

"But you're my boss," she breathed, clutching his shirt collar with a death grip. But her bright, luminous green eyes gazed up at him. And those eyes said yes.

Her lips were plush, parted, eager for his. He brought his thumb back to scrape them. "Just pretend I'm not him."

"But you *are* him—"

"I don't want to be him, I want to be…just Marcos." Their relationship had been wrapped in rules, limited by their roles. What if Virginia had been just a woman? And he just a man? She would have been his, might still be his. "Only Marcos."

The passing city lights caused slanted shadows to shift across her face—she looked splendid, wary, wanting.

"A kiss is harmless, Virginia." His vision blurred with desire as he stretched his arm out on the seat behind her and dipped his head. Their breaths mingled, their mouths opened. "People kiss their pets. They kiss their enemies on the cheeks. They kiss a letter. They even blow kisses into the air. You can kiss me."

"This is a little unexpected."

"God, I'd hate to be predictable." His arm slid from the back of the seat and went around her shoulders, loosely holding her to him. His fingers played with the soft, bouncy curls at her nape. His accent got unbearably thick—like his blood, a terse string of lust flooding his veins. It took concentration to give her a smile meant to disarm. "Stop thinking about it and kiss me."

Her curls bounced at the shake of her head. "We don't have to kiss to pretend to be…together. I can pretend convincingly without kissing."

No kissing? Christ, no. He had a fascination with her mouth, the delicate bow at her upper lip, the ripe flesh of the bottom one. He'd been kissing that mouth for days, weeks, months, in his mind.

"You're wrong, *amor.*" He bussed her temple with his lips, aware of his muscles flexing heatedly under his clothes, his skin feverish with pent-up desire as she continued clinging to his shirt. "We must kiss. And we must kiss convincingly."

"I— You didn't mention this before."

He caressed her cheekbone with the back of one finger and noted the frantic pulse fluttering at the base of her throat. Christ, once again she was fixated with his mouth, and he wanted to give it to her. Now. Right now. Slam it over hers, push into her, taste all of her. "Kiss me, Virginia. Kiss me senseless." He barely held himself in check with his ruthless self-discipline.

She hesitated. Then, in a burdened breath, "Only a kiss."

His heart rammed into his ribs at the realization that she had agreed. To kiss him. *Ay, Dios.*

He urged himself to ease back on the seat and stifled the impulse to take matters into his own hands. He was a second away from losing his mind. A second away from tearing off her clothes, the necklace at her throat, his shirt, everything that separated them. Still, he wanted to be sure, sure she wanted this. Him. Them.

He groaned and said, "Kiss me until we can't breathe."

"I... The driver could see us." She sounded as excited as he, and the breathless anticipation in her voice plunged him even deeper into wild, mad desire.

"Look at me, not him."

"You're all I'm looking at, Marcos."

He didn't know who breathed harder, who was seducing whom here. She laid her hands over his abdomen. He hissed. The muscles under her palms clenched. His erection strained painfully.

Her hands slid up his chest, a barely there touch. *Fever.* She cradled his jaw with two cool, dry palms...and waited. Hesitant, inexperienced. In a ragged plea, she croaked, "Close your eyes."

He did. Not because she asked, but because her fingers lovingly stroked his temple, down his jaw. Her hands drifted lower and curled around his shoulders, rubbing along the muscles so sensually he gritted his teeth. This was murder.

She had to stop. She had to go on.

"Do it. Do it now." The helpless urgency in his voice startled him as much as the other emotions coursing through him. Arousal ripped through him like a living beast.

Then he felt the warm mist of her breath on his face, sensed the nearness of her parting lips, heard through the roaring in his ears her tremulous whisper. "I'm a bit out of practice—"

He didn't let her finish. He reached out and slipped a hand beneath the fall of hair at her nape and hauled her to him. "Virginia," he rasped, and slammed her mouth with his.

Four

Virginia had meant for a quick kiss. Only a taste. A taste to satisfy her curiosity. Her need. A taste because she could not, could never, deny this man. But when he pulled her down and his mouth, so strong and fierce and hungry, touched hers, there was no stopping what came over her.

They'd been panting, laughing; he'd been teasing her, had pulled her onto his lap. Pretending had been so easy, but now…now this mouth, this man, the hands gripping the back of her head, were too real. Rough. Raw. Devastating.

She moaned helplessly as he slanted his head, murmuring something indiscernible to her, and his warm, hot tongue came at hers, and his hard need grew larger and stronger under her bottom, and the realization that he really *wanted her* barraged through her.

He began to take little nips, and those lush, sure lips moving against hers set off the flutters in her stomach, the fireworks in her head. *"Sabes a miel."*

He spoke in an aroused rasp against her lips. She clung to

his neck and tried not to moan as his warm breath slid across her skin, heating her like a fever.

"Te quiero hacer el amor," he murmured, running his hands down the sides of her body, his fingers brushing the curves of her breasts, his chest heaving with exerted restraint. *"Toda la noche, te quiero hacer el amor."*

She had no idea what he said, but the words pulsed through her in a wave of erotic pleasure. Her breasts swelled heavy, her nipples in such pain she pressed them deeper into his chest and she opened her mouth wide, moving instinctively against him, and she knew this was wrong, so wrong, would not happen again, which surely must be why she incited it. "What are you saying to me..." she murmured into him.

His breath was hot and rapid against her. "I'm saying I want to make love to you. All evening, all night." He groaned and twisted his tongue around hers as their lips locked, the attachment intense, driven, absolute.

She sucked in a breath as his palms engulfed her straining nipples, felt his desire in every coiled muscle, in the rough way his palms kneaded, the thrusts of his tongue as his mouth turned ravenous on hers.

He groaned, appearing decidedly out of control for the first time since she'd known him. He stroked the undersides of her breasts with his thumbs and whisked his lips along the curve of her jaw, and she cocked her ear to his nibbling lips, shuddered when he murmured to her. "Your gasps tear me to pieces."

"Marcos..."

She was hot and burning inside.

He made a grinding motion with his hips, and her thighs splayed open as he desperately rubbed his erection against her.

His tongue plunged into her ear, wet, hot, sloppy. "Stop me, Virginia." One determined hand unerringly slipped through the V of her dress and enveloped her breast. "Virginia. Stop me, Virginia."

He squeezed her flesh possessively, and when his palm rubbed into her nipple, her eyes flew open in shock. The feel was so delicious, so wrong, so *right,* she hid her heated face against his neck and almost choked on the sounds welling at the back of her throat. Sensations overpowered her body, her mind struggling to comprehend that this was really happening with Marcos Allende.

"That's your hotel up ahead, sir."

Swearing under his breath, Marcos gathered her closer. His ragged breaths blasted her temple. He squeezed her. "We'll finish this upstairs."

Virginia pushed back her rumpled hair. Upstairs? God, what were they even doing?

Chuckling at the look on her face, Marcos bussed her forehead with his lips as his gentle hand stroked down her nape, trembling slightly. "I should've known we'd be combustible," he murmured.

The Mercedes pulled into a wide, palm tree–lined hotel driveway and Virginia fumbled for her purse while Marcos stepped out and strolled to her side, reaching into the car and helping her to her feet.

His glimmering, dark gaze didn't stray from her face, not for a second. *We kissed,* his dark eyes said. *I touched you. I know you want me.*

And for an insane second, all she wanted was to forget why she was here and who she was and be swept away by this one man, this one night, in this one city.

As though discerning her thoughts, Marcos cupped half of her face in his warm palm, and his eyes held something so wild and bright it almost blinded her. "Upstairs," he said again.

The promise plunged into her like a knife as he moved away to discuss something with the chauffeur, and Virginia stood there like someone in a hypnotized state, watching his big, tanned hands at his sides. Hands she'd felt on her.

She gritted her teeth, fighting the lingering arousal tickling through her. He was playing with her. He was *pretending*. He was a man who'd do anything to win—and he wanted Allende.

Marcos seemed oblivious to her frustration when he returned, slowly reaching behind her, his fingers splaying over the small of her back as he led her up the steps.

She followed him and no, she wasn't imagining him naked, touching her, kissing her in the exact way he'd just done—no, no, no. She studied the beautiful hotel and the potted palms leading to the glass doors with the intensity of a scientist with his microscope.

The lobby and its domed ceiling made her lightheaded. It was so…so… God, the way he'd touched her. With those hands. As if that breast were his to touch and his hand belonged there. How could he pretend so well? He'd been so hard he could've broken cement with his…his…

"Do you like it, Virginia?" he asked, smiling, and signaled around.

She gazed at the elegant but rustic decor. "The hotel? It's beautiful."

His eyes twinkled, but underneath it all, he wore the starved look of a man who'd hungered for a very long time and intended to feast soon. He looked like a man who could do things to her she didn't even imagine in fantasies, like a man who would not want to be denied.

And he would be. He had to be.

"It's very…charming," she continued, anything to steer her mind away from his lips, his mouth, his gaze.

They wound deeper into the marbled hotel lobby. A colorful flower arrangement boasting the most enormous sunflowers she'd ever seen sat on a massive round table near the reception area.

Virginia could still not account, could not even fathom, that she'd just kissed him. Her!—woefully inexperienced, with her last boyfriend dating back to college—kissing Marcos Allende. But he'd been cuddling her, whispering words so naughty she could hardly stand the wanton warmth they elicited. No matter how much resistance she'd tried to put up, he was the sexiest thing on the continent, playing some sort of grown-up game she had yet to put a name to, and Virginia had been close to a meltdown.

It had all been pretend, anyway. Right?

Right.

Trying to compose herself, she admired his broad back as he strolled away, the shoulders straining under his black shirt as he reached the reception desk and leaned over with confidence, acting for the world as if he were the majority stockholder of the hotel. The two women shuffling behind the granite top treated him as if they agreed.

Virginia quietly drew up to his side, her lips feeling raw and sensitive. She licked them once, twice.

A lock of ebony hair fell over Marcos's forehead as he signed the slip and slid it over the counter. "I requested a two-bedroom suite—it would appease me to know you're safe. Will this be a problem?" Facing her, he plunged his Montblanc pen into his shirt pocket, watching her through calm, assessing eyes.

She saw protectiveness there, concern, and though her nerves protested by twisting, she said, "Not at all." Damn. What hell to keep pretending for a week.

"Good."

In the elevator, as they rode up to the ninth floor—the top floor of the low, sprawling building—his body big and commanding in the constricted space, the silence whispered, *we kissed.*

In her mind, her heart, the choir of her reason, everything said, *kiss kiss kiss.*

Not good, any of it. Not the blender her emotions were in, not her tilting world, not the fact that she was already thinking, anticipating, wondering, what it would feel like to kiss again.

Freely. Wildly. Without restraint.

She would have to stall. Abstain. Ignore him. God. If she did something to compromise her job, she would never forgive herself. And nothing compromised a job like sex did. And if she compromised her heart? She stiffened, firmly putting a lid on the thought.

Mom had loved Dad with all her heart—through his flaws, through his odd humors, through his drunken nights, through all the good and bad of which there was more of the latter, her mother had loved with such steadfast, blinded devotion Virginia had secretly felt...pity.

Because her mother had wept more tears for a man than a human should be allowed to weep. Appalling, that one man could have such power over a woman, could take her heart and her future and trample them without thought or conscience.

Even on her deathbed, sweet, beautiful, dedicated Mother had clutched Virginia's hand, and it seemed she'd been hanging on to her life only to continue trying to save her husband. "Take care of Dad, Virginia, he needs someone to look out for him. Promise me, baby? Promise me you will?"

Virginia had promised, determinedly telling herself that if she ever, ever gave away her heart, it would be to someone who would be reliable, and who loved her more than his cards, his games and himself.

No matter her physical, shockingly visceral responses to Marcos, he was still everything she should be wary of. Worldly, sophisticated, ruthless, a man enamored of a challenge, of risks and of his job. The last thing she pictured

Marcos Allende being was a family man, no matter how generous he'd proven to be as a boss.

Down the hall, the bellhop emerged from the service elevator, but Marcos was already trying his key, allowing her inside. He flicked on the light switch and the suite glowed in welcome. Golden-tapestried walls, plush taupe-colored carpet, a large sitting area opening up to a room on each side. *"Gracias,"* he said, tipping the bellhop at the door and personally hauling both suitcases inside.

Virginia surveyed the mouthwatering array of food atop the coffee table: trays of chocolate-dipped strawberries, sliced fruit, imported cheeses.

A newspaper sat next to the silver trays and the word *muerte* popped out in the headline. A color picture of a tower of mutilated people stared back at her.

Marcos deadbolted the door. The sound almost made her wince. And she realized how alone they were. Just him. And her.

And their plan.

Suddenly and with all her might, Virginia wished to know what he was thinking. Did he think they'd kiss again? What if he wanted more than a kiss? What if he didn't?

Feeling her skin pebble, she shied away from his gaze, navigated around a set of chairs and pulled the sheer drapes aside. The city flickered with lights. Outside her window the hotel pool was eerily still, the mountains were still, the moon still. She noted the slow, rough curves and the sharper turns at the peaks, lifted her hand to trace them on the glass. "Do you come here frequently?" she asked quietly—her insides were not still.

"No." She heard the sunken fall of his footsteps on the carpet as he approached—she felt, rather than saw, him draw up behind her. "There wasn't reason to."

He could be uttering something else for the way he spoke so intimately. Inside, a rope of wanting stretched taut around her stomach and she thought she would faint. The proximity of his broad, unyielding hardness sent a flood of warmth across her body, and the muscles of her tummy clenched with yearning. His body wasn't touching hers; there was just the threat of the touch, the presence that created a wanting of it.

In the darkness of her bedroom, very late at night, she'd wondered if Marcos was as ruthless when he loved as when he did business. And if his kiss...was as dark and devastating as his eyes had promised it would be.

It was. Oh, God, it was.

The air seemed to scream at her to turn to him and *kiss*.

The close contours of his chest against her back, the scent of him, were an assault to her senses. He laid his hand on her shoulder, and the touch was fire on his fingertips. "This is a safe neighborhood—I won't lose sight of you, Virginia."

But outside the danger didn't lurk. It was in her. It was him. She locked her muscles in place, afraid of leaning, moving, afraid of the magnetic force of him, how it felt impossible not to turn, touch. "What was it like for you when you were young," she said, softly.

His hand stroked. Fire streaked across her skin as he drew lazy figures along the back of her arm. "It wasn't as dangerous back then. I grew up in the streets—I kept running away with my father's workers, looking for adventure."

Did he move? She thought he'd grown bigger, harder, nearer. She sensed his arousal, the thundering in his chest almost touching her back. Or was it her heart she heard?

He lowered his lips and briefly, only a whisper, set his mouth on her neck. A sharp shudder rushed through her. "Now even bodyguards aren't safe to hire," he whispered on her skin. "Wealthy people have armored cars and weapons instead."

She closed her eyes, the sensations pouring through her.

"No-man's-land?" Just a croak. A peep from a little bird who couldn't fly, would willingly be lured in by the feline.

He made a pained sound and stilled his movements on her. "Were you pretending just now when you kissed me?"

Oh. My. God. They were actually discussing it.

Her nod was jerky.

Marcos hesitated, then huskily murmured, "Do you want to…?"

She sank her teeth into her lower lip to keep from saying something stupid, like yes. "To what?"

His whisper tumbled down her ear. "You know what."

"I don't know what you mean." But she did. Oh, dear, she did.

"Kiss…" Thick and terse, his voice brimmed with passion. "Touch…"

Shaking like a leaf in a storm, she wiggled free and walked around him, her insides wrenching. "I told you I could pretend just fine."

Heading for the couch and plopping down, she surveyed the food once more, but her eyes didn't see anything.

Was she supposed to stay strong and resist what her body and heart wanted when she had a chance to have it? Was she supposed to say no and no and no?

Marcos plunged his hand into his hair. "That was *pretense?*"

"Of course." He sounded so shocked and looked so annoyed she might have even laughed. Instead, her voice grew businesslike. "So you left. And your father stayed here? In this city?"

For a moment, he released a cynical laugh, and when he gradually recovered, he roughly scraped the back of his hand across his mouth as if he couldn't stand remembering their kiss. Reluctantly, he nodded. "You're good, Miss Hollis, I'll give you that."

"What made you leave here?" she asked, blinking.

One lone eyebrow rose and this time when he laughed, she knew it was at her attempt at conversation.

"Well." Propping a shoulder against the wall and crossing his arms over his chest in a seemingly relaxed pose, Marcos exuded a raw, primal power that seemed to take command of the entire room. "Allende Transport was taken. By my father's…woman. It was either her or me—and he chose her. But I promised myself when I came back…the transport company would be mine."

His voice. Sometimes she'd hear it, not the words, just the bass, the accent. Marcos was larger than life, large in every single way, and Virginia could pretend all she wanted but the fact was, she'd be stupid to forget her position. And she had to make sure the car incident would never again be repeated.

"Marcos, what happened here and in the car was—"

"Only the beginning."

She started. The beginning of what? The end? She ground her molars, fighting for calm. "We were pretending."

"Aha."

"Yes," she said, vehemently. "We were."

"Right, Miss Hollis. Whatever you say."

"You asked me to pretend, that's what I'm here for. Isn't it?"

His silence was so prolonged she felt deafened. Was she here for another reason? A reason other than what he'd requested of her? An intimate, wicked, naughty reason?

She could tell by the set of his jaw that if he had a hidden agenda, he wouldn't be admitting to it now.

Walking off her conflicting emotions, she fixed her attention on the food. The scents of lemon, warm bread, cheeses and fruit teased her nostrils, but her stomach was too constricted for her to summon any appetite. Usually she'd be wolfing down the strawberries, but now she wiped her hands on her sides and put on her best secretarial face. "At what time should I wake up tomorrow?"

"We have a late lunch, no need to rise with the sun," he said.

She signaled to both ends of the room, needing to get away from him, wishing she could get away from herself. "And my room?"

"Pick the one you like."

She felt his gaze on her, sensed it like a fiery lick across her skin.

She went over and peered into a room: a large, double-post bed, white and blue bedclothes. Very beautiful. She went to the other, feeling his eyes follow. The lamplight cast his face in beautiful mellow light. He looked like an angel that had just escaped from hell, like an angel she wanted to sin with.

"I guess either will do," she admitted.

She smiled briefly at him from the doorway, and although he returned the smile, both smiles seemed empty.

And in that instant Virginia was struck with two things at once: she had never wanted anything so much in her life as she wanted the man standing before her, and if his lips covered hers again, if his hands touched her, if his eyes continued to look at her, she would never own her heart again.

She said, "Good night." And didn't wait to hear his reply.

The room she chose was the one with coral-pink bedding and an upholstered headboard. She didn't question that, for appearances, he would wish him and his "lover" to appear to share a room. But she quietly turned the lock behind her.

As she changed, she thought of what she had read about Marcos and Monterrey. She arranged the clothes in the large closet, each garment on a hanger, and eyed and touched the ones he'd bought her.

She slipped into her cotton nightgown, ignoring the prettier garments made of silk and satin and lace, and climbed into bed. Awareness of his proximity in the adjoining room caused gooseflesh along her arms. A fan hung suspended from the ceiling, twirling. The echo of his words feathered through her, melting her bones. *I'll pretend...you're her.*

She squeezed her eyes shut, her chest constricting. *It's not you, Virginia,* she firmly told herself.

She touched a finger against her sensitive lips and felt a lingering pleasure. And in her heart of hearts, she knew she was. She was her, the woman Marcos wanted. She'd dreamed of him in private, but dreams had been so harmless until they came within reach.

Marcos Allende.

Wanting him was the least safe, most staggering, worrying feeling she'd ever felt.

And one thing she knew for certain was that to her, Marcos Allende was even more dangerous than his beautiful, deadly city of Monterrey.

Sleep eluded him.

The clock read past 1:00 a.m. and Marcos had smashed his pillow into a beat-up ball. He'd kicked off the covers. He'd cursed and then he'd cursed himself some more for thinking one kiss would be enough to rid himself of his obsession of her.

Then there was Allende.

He had to plan, plot, leave no room for error. He had to stoke his hatred of Marissa, to be prepared to crush her once and for all.

But he could not think of anything. Memories of those kisses in the car assailed him. The fierce manner in which his mouth took hers and her greedy responses, the moans she let out when he'd touched her. How his tongue had taken hers, how she'd groaned those tormenting sounds.

He lay awake and glared at the ceiling, his mind counting the steps to her room. Twenty? Maybe fewer. Was she asleep? What did she wear to sleep? Was she remembering, too? Jesus, what a nightmare.

He shouldn't have asked her there.

He'd thought nothing of Allende, nothing of tomorrow, but had kept going over in his mind the ways she'd kissed him and the ways he still wanted to kiss her.

He sat up and critically surveyed the door of his room. He wanted her to give in. Wanted something of hers, a stolen moment, something she hadn't planned to give him, but couldn't help but relinquish. She was cautious by nature. She'd fear ruining everything, all she'd worked so hard for, all she'd tried to achieve. A steady job, security, respect. Could he guarantee this would remain solid when they were through? Could they even continue working together—flaring up like torches like this?

Their kiss had shot him up into outer space; obviously he still couldn't think right. In his drawstring pants, he climbed out of bed and slipped into his shirt.

He meant to review his numbers once again, ascertain that the amount he planned to offer for Allende was low, but fair enough to secure it.

Instead he ignored his files and found himself standing outside his assistant's bedroom door, his hand on the doorknob, his heart beating a crazy jungle-cat rhythm.

He turned the knob, smiling at his certainty of her, her being always so…orderly, having locked it against him.

His heart stopped when he realized Virginia Hollis's door was unlocked. Now all that kept him from Virginia Hollis were his damned scruples.

Five

"Sleep well?"

"Of course. Wonderfully well. And you?"

"Perfectly."

That was the extent of their conversation the next morning over breakfast. Until Marcos began folding his copy of *El Norte*. "A favor from you, Miss Hollis?"

Virginia glanced up from her breakfast to stare into his handsome, clean-shaven face. *A kiss,* she thought with a tightness in her stomach. A touch. God, a second kiss to get rid of that haunting memory of the first.

With her thoughts presenting her the image of him— Marcos Allende—kissing her, she flushed so hard her skin felt on fire. She toyed with her French toast. "Nothing too drastic, I assume?" she said, some of the giddiness she felt creeping into her voice.

"Drastic?" he repeated, setting the morning paper aside.

She shrugged. "Oh, you know…murder. Blackmail. I don't think I could get away with those."

Eyes glinting with amusement, he shook his head, and his smile was gone. His elbows came to rest on the table as he leaned forward. "What kind of boss do you take me for?"

One I want, she thought. *One who kissed me.*

Those broad, rippling muscles under his shirt could belong to a warrior.

God just didn't make men like these anymore.

She'd lied. She hadn't slept one wink.

If she'd been camping out in the dark, naked, within ten feet of a hungry lion, maybe she'd have been able to sleep. But no. She had been within a few feet of her dream man, and her lips had still tingled from his kiss, and her body seemed to scream for all the years she hadn't paid attention to letting someone love it.

After lying on the bed for what felt like hours, for some strange reason she had bolted to her feet and rummaged through the stuff he'd bought…and slipped into something sexy. A sleek white silk gown that hugged her like skin. Heart vaulting in excitement, she'd unlocked the door. Returned to bed. And waited. Eyeing the door.

The knob had begun turning. Her eyes widened, and her pulse went out of orbit. She waited minutes, minutes, for the door to open, and yet the knob returned to place again. Nothing happened. He changed his mind? Her heart sped, and then she flung off the covers and stepped out of bed.

The living room was empty—silver in the moonlight. And then, torn between some unnamable need and the need for self-preservation, she'd quietly gone back to bed.

Now, looking like a well-rested, sexy billionaire, he asked what kind of boss she took him for.

"One who's never bitten me," she blurted, then wished to kick herself for the way that came out sounding. Like an invitation. Like…more. Damn him.

He chuckled instantly, and Virginia pushed to her feet

when she totally lost her appetite. He followed her up, uncurling slowly like he always did.

"I like the dress," he said, studying the fabric as it molded around her curves. It was a very nice dress. Green, to match her eyes, and one from a designer to please His Majesty.

"Thank you, I like it, too."

His gaze raked her so intimately she felt stripped to her skin. There was a silence. Her heart pounded once. Twice. Three times. Virginia couldn't take a fourth.

"Name your favor," she offered.

Eyes locked with hers with unsettling intensity, he wound around the table, and his scent enveloped her—not of cologne and definitely not sweet—but so intoxicating she wanted to inhale until her lungs burst inside her chest.

Gently, he seized her chin between his thumb and forefinger, tipping his face back to hers. An unnamable darkness eclipsed his eyes, and an unprecedented huskiness crept into his voice. "Just say, 'Yes, Marcos.'"

Her breath caught. His voice was so ridiculously sexy in the morning. Virginia pulled free of his touch and laughed. "You," she accused, tingles dancing across her skin. "I don't even know what I'm agreeing to."

His arms went around her, slow as a boa constrictor, securing her like giant manacles. "Can't you guess?"

Something exploded inside her body, and it wasn't fear. Lust. Desire. Everything she didn't want to feel.

His breath was hot and fragrant on her face, eliciting a little moan she couldn't contain. Oh, God. He felt so hard all over, so unlike any other man she'd known.

His voice was gentle as he tipped her chin up. "Yes to my bed for a week, Virginia. Say yes."

Was he insane? "Wow," she said, almost choking on her shock. "I've never had such a blatant come-on."

The determination on his face was anything but apologetic. "I don't want to play games with you." He studied her forehead, her nose, her jaw. "I intend to please you. I've thought of nothing else. Tell me," he urged, caressing her face as he would a porcelain sculpture. "Are you interested?"

Interested? She was on fire, she was frightened, confused and scared, and she hated thinking, realizing that she was no match for him.

She should've known that if Marcos ever made a move for her, he'd come on like he always did—strong, like a stampeding bull charging to get his way. Her breasts rose and fell against his chest as she labored to breathe. Her legs were so weak they couldn't support her, and she remained standing only by her deathly grip on his arms. "One week?"

"Seven days. Seven nights. Of pleasure beyond your imagining."

"A-and what if I can't give you this pleasure you want?"

"I will take any pleasure you can give me, Virginia. And you will take mine."

There was no mistaking. His deep, sexy voice was the most erotic thing she'd ever heard. "A-and if I say I'm not interested?"

He chuckled softly—the sound throaty, arrogant, male—melting her defenses. "If that is what you wish." His gaze pierced her, as though searching for secrets, fears. "You haven't wondered about us?" He lowered his head and skimmed her lips lightly, enough to tease and make her shiver when he retracted. "You unlocked your door last night, and I was so close to opening it, you have no idea."

"Oh, God," she breathed.

His lips grazed hers from end to end. "You wanted me there, you wanted me in your room, your bed."

"I—I can't do this."

His hands lowered to the small of her back and pressed her to his warm, solid length. "You can. Your body speaks to me. It feels soft against mine, it molds to me. Say it in words."

There was no escaping his powerful stare, no escape from what raged inside her. "I can't, Marcos."

Growling, he jerked free and for a blinding second she thought he was going to charge out of the room, he seemed so frustrated. Instead he carried himself—six feet three inches of testosterone and lust and anger—to the window and leaned on the frame. "The first moment I set eyes on you, you planted yourself in my mind. I'm going insane because once, Virginia, once I was sure you were crazy about me. So crazy. You can't help the way you look at me, *amor*. Perhaps others don't notice, but I do. Why do you fight me?"

Her eyes flicked up to his and she was certain her anxiety reached out to him like something tangible. His muscles went taut. "Do I get an answer?" he demanded.

She smiled, shaking her head in disbelief. "You're proposing we mix business and pleasure."

He wanted her desperately, she realized. Like she'd never been wanted before. And she might enjoy allowing herself to be wanted like this.

So, with a pang of anticipation in her left breast, she said, "I'll think about it over lunch."

The floral arrangement in the lobby had been replaced with one chock-full of red gerberas and bright orange tiger lilies bursting amidst green. They navigated around it, Marcos's hand on her back.

"If you want everyone to know you're nervous, by all means, keep fidgeting."

"Fidgeting? Who's fidgeting?"

He grabbed her trembling hand and linked his fingers through hers, his smile more like a grin. "Now no one. Smile, hmm? Pretend you like me."

Her pulse skyrocketed at the feel of his palm against hers, but she did not reject the touch and held on. *This should be easy. Easy,* she told herself. One look at her and everyone would think she was in love with him.

Impulsively she breathed him in, feeling oddly safe and protected. They'd had a wonderful morning, talking of everything and nothing as he accompanied her to the shopping mall across the street. The morning had flown by in casual conversation, which had been a good thing particularly when the night had seemed endless to her.

Now they entered the restaurant. Past the arched foyer entrance stood the most beautiful woman Virginia had ever seen. Tall and toned, blonde and beautiful. Her lips were red, her nails were red. She was clad in a short leather jacket teamed with a white miniskirt and a pair of heels Virginia was certain only an acrobat could walk on. Her face lit up like a sunbeam when she saw Marcos, and then it eclipsed when she saw Virginia.

She swept to her feet and came to them, her walk as graceful as the swaying of a willow tree. All other female eyes in the restaurant landed on Marcos.

"You're bigger." Her eyes became shielded, wary when they moved to her. "And you're…not alone."

In one clean sweep, Marissa took in the entire length of Virginia's knee-length emerald-green designer dress.

Marcos drew her up closer to him and brought those inscrutable eyes of his down on Virginia, his gaze sharpening possessively. "Virginia Hollis, Marissa Galvez."

He gave Virginia such a male, proprietary look she felt stirrings in all manner of places in her body. Nervous, she offered the woman a nod and a smile. Marissa's hand was slim and ringed everywhere. They shook hands and took their seats.

The awkwardness had a strange beat—slower somehow, and heavy like lead.

Over the sunlit table, Virginia tentatively slid her hand into Marcos's, sensed him smile to himself, then felt him give her a squeeze of gratitude which Marissa might have taken as affection. A silence settled. Every minute was a little more agonizing. Marcos's thumb began to stroke the back of hers, causing pinpricks of awareness to trail up her arm. Sensations of wanting tumbled, one after the other. What would it be like if this were real? Sitting here, with such a man, and knowing the name of the shampoo he showered with and the cologne he wore?

Marissa's blue eyes shone with a tumult of emotions. "Why didn't you come to him? He begged you to."

Virginia's spine stiffened. Whoa. That had been quite a hostile opening line. But then what did she know?

Marcos answered coolly, reclining easily in his upholstered chair. "I did come."

"A day too late."

The corners of his lips kicked up, but the smile was hard somehow, and it didn't reach his eyes. The air was so tense and dense it was scarcely breathable. "Perhaps if he'd really sent for me, I'd have come sooner—but we both know it wasn't him who summoned me."

Surprise flickered across the blonde's face. "Why would he not call his son on his deathbed?"

"Because he's an Allende."

She made a noncommittal sound, rings flashing as she reclined her chin on her right hand. Her eyes dropped to Virginia and Marcos's locked hands over the table, and finally the woman shrugged. "He died with his pride—but I could see him watching the door every day. He wanted to see you. Every time I came in he…" She faltered, pain flashing across her face as she lowered her arm. "He looked away."

Marcos was idly playing with Virginia's fingers. Did he realize? It seemed to distract him. Comfort him, maybe. "He didn't want to see you, Marissa?"

Her eyes became glimmering blue slits. "He wasn't

himself those last days." She smiled tightly. *"No se que le paso, estaba muy raro."*

Even as Marcos replied in that calm, controlled voice, Virginia sensed his will there, incontestable, allowing for nothing. "You ruin your life for a woman—I suppose you're bound to have regrets. And to be acting strange," he added, as though referencing the words she's said in Spanish.

A waiter dressed in black and white took their orders. Virginia ordered what Marcos was having, wishing she could try everything on the menu at least once but embarrassed to show herself as a glutton. When the waiter moved on, Marissa's eyes wandered over her. She tapped one long red fingernail to the corners of her red lips.

"You don't look like Marcos's type at all," she commented matter-of-factly.

Virginia half turned to him for a hint of how to answer, and he lifted her hand to graze her knuckles with his lips, saying in a playful murmur that only she seemed to hear, "Aren't you glad to hear that, *amor?*"

She shivered in primal, feminine response to the smooth touch of his lips, and impulsively stroked her fingers down his face. "You didn't see your father before he died?" she asked quietly.

His eyes darkened with emotion. "No," he said, and this time when he kissed the back of her hand, he did so lingeringly, holding her gaze. Her temperature jacked up; how did he do this to her?

The moment when he spread her hand open so her palm cupped his jaw, it felt like it was just them. Nobody else in the restaurant, the hotel, the world.

"You'd never abandon your father," he murmured as he held her gaze trapped, pressing her palm against his face. "I admire that."

Her chest moved as if pulled by an invisible string toward him. Had she ever received a more flattering compliment?

His pain streaked through her as though she'd adopted it as hers, and she ached to make him feel better, to take the darkness away from his eyes, to kiss him…kiss him all over.

She stroked his rough jaw with her fingers instead, unable to stop herself. "Perhaps he knew you loved him, and he understood you kept to your pride, like he did," she suggested.

"Marcos? Love? He wouldn't know love if it trampled him," Marissa scoffed and frowned at Marcos, then sobered up when he swiveled around to send her a chilling look. "It's my fault anyway. That you left. I've paid dearly for my mistake, I guarantee it," she added.

He didn't reply. His gaze had dropped to where his thumb stroked the back of Virginia's hand again, distracting her from the conversation that ensued. He seemed to prefer that touch above anything else. He kept stroking, caressing, moving her hand places. He put it, with his, over his thigh, or tucked it under his arm. Longing speared through her every single time he moved it according to his will. He genuinely seemed to…want it. Was he pretending? When his eyes came to hers, there was such warmth and heat there.… Was he pretending that, too?

Marissa mentioned Allende, and Marcos, prepared for the discussion, immediately answered. His voice stroked down Virginia's spine every time he spoke. Her reaction was the same: a shudder, a quiver, a pang. And she didn't want it to be. She didn't want to have a reaction, she shouldn't.

While the waiter set down their meals, she thought of her father, of how many times he'd disappointed and angered her, and she thought of how hurt she'd have to be in order not to see him again. Sometimes she'd wanted to leave, to pretend he didn't exist to her, and those times, she would feel like the worst sort of daughter for entertaining those thoughts.

Marcos wasn't a heartless man. He stuck by his brother

no matter what he did. *My brother is a person, Allende is not,* he'd told her. But his father had been a person, too. What had he done to Marcos to warrant such anger?

She had her answer fifteen minutes later, after she'd eaten the most spicy chile relleno on the continent and swallowed five full glasses of water to prove it. She excused herself to the *baño* and was about to return to the table when she heard Marissa's plea from the nearby table filter into the narrow corridor. "Marcos…if you'd only give me a chance…"

"I'm here to discuss Allende. Not your romps in my father's bed."

"Marcos, I was young, and he was so…so powerful, so interested in me in a way you never were. You were never asking me to marry you, never!"

He didn't answer that. Virginia hadn't realized she stood frozen until a waiter came to ask if she was all right. She nodded, but couldn't make her legs start for the table yet. Her chest hurt so acutely she thought someone had just pulled out her lungs. Marissa Galvez and Marcos. So it was because of a woman, because of her, that Marcos had never spoken again to his father?

"You never once told me if you cared for me, while he… he cared. He wanted me more than anything." Marissa trailed off as if she'd noticed Marcos wasn't interested in her conversation. "So who is this woman? She's a little simple for you—no?"

He laughed, genuinely laughed. "Virginia? Simple?"

Virginia heard her answering whisper, too low to discern, and then she heard his, also too low, and something horrible went through her, blinding her eyes, sinking its claws into her. She remembered how difficult it was as a little girl to cope with the whispers.

The father is always gambling…they say he's crazy…

Now they talked about her. Not about her father. About her. She didn't hear what he said, or what she said, only felt the pain and humiliation slicing through her. Her father had put her in this position once more. No. She'd put herself in it. Pretending to be lovers with a man she truly, desperately wanted…and then looking the fool in front of someone she was sure had really been his lover.

Jealousy swelled and rose in her. She had no right to feel it, had never been promised anything, and yet she did feel it. Their kiss yesterday had been glorified in her mind and she'd begun to wishfully think Marcos had wanted to be with her this week. Silly. She'd even told herself she might like sharing his bed for a week.

She felt winded and strangely stiff when she reached the table. She sat quietly. She focused on dessert, tried to taste and enjoy, and yet her anger mounted, as if she really were his lover, as if she had anything to claim of him.

When he reached for her hand, it took all her effort, it took her every memory of having gone to beg him for help that evening, not to pull it away.

If she weren't sitting she'd be kicking herself for being so easy. She sucked in air then held it as he guided that hand to his mouth and grazed her knuckles with his lips.

Her racing heart begged for more, but Marcos's kiss was less obvious than last night, more like a whisper on her skin. Every grazing kiss he gave each knuckle felt like a stroke in her core.

A slap in the face.

They say her father's crazy…

By all means, Virginia would pull her hand away in a few seconds. She just wanted…more. More hot breath and warm lips on the back of her hand. More fire between her legs. A place so hot and moist it could only be cooled by—

Something moved.

His phone.

His lips paused on her for a breathless second before he

set her hand back on her lap and whispered, "It's the office. I have to get this."

Virginia made a strangled sound which was supposed to be an agreement and clearly sounded more like a dying woman. She watched his dark silhouette move between the tables and disappear down the hall so quickly. She already missed him. She scanned her surroundings. Everybody was eating, carrying on conversations. The world hadn't stopped like she'd thought because of those tiny kisses on her knuckles.

She sank back in her seat, agitated when Marissa watched her. She brought her hand to her mouth, the one he'd kissed, and closed her eyes as she grazed her lips in the exact same places his lips had touched.

Eyes popping open to meet the other woman's canny gaze, she straightened, readjusted the hem of her knee-length dress, and mentally cursed this pretense from here to Alaska and then to Mars. Was he seducing her? Or was this all for Marissa's sake?

"So," Marissa said. "You love him."

Virginia was about to jump in denial, frantic to save herself from this accusation, which of course implied that she was stupid, needed therapy and more, and then she realized he was counting on her to pretend that she did.

Love him.

"I…" Her lips couldn't form the words *I love him*. Her tongue seemed to freeze. Seemed to want to say only one thing, and that was *I hate him*.

She hated him and this stupid plan and how he touched her and how well he pretended to want her.

So instead she nodded, and let Marissa think what she would.

His powerful scent reached her long before he sat down beside her again. Virginia stared straight ahead like a horse with blinders. And just to prevent any more stoking of the staggering anger building inside her, she tucked her hands under her thighs. There. See if the man could touch her knuckles now.

She remained quiet the rest of the meal.

She heard Marissa invite them to a party the next day while she considered Marcos's offer.

She told herself she didn't care to know what kind of offer he'd made.

Six

Something had changed.

Virginia had changed. She was different, and yet, it was all the same with him. The twisting sensation in his gut, the demented beat of his heart, the itch in his hands, the coiling want in his body.

Alert, clever, perceptive and spirited…now his assistant seemed to be struggling to comprehend what she'd witnessed as they reached their rooms.

They'd had such an enjoyable time this morning, he'd been certain he knew where they were heading tonight.

He wasn't sure anymore.

He wasn't sure of anything—very unlike an Allende.

He took her to the middle of the living room and just stood there, his jacket in one hand, looking at her. His every muscle felt stiff and pained, his hard-on merciless, and when he moved the slightest bit, arousal lanced through him. He set his jacket aside and felt as if the air was being squeezed out of his lungs. She was disappointed he'd been such a bad son to his father? He'd lost her admiration? Her respect?

His insides twisted at the thought. He stepped forward, toward her, his thoughts congested, tangled like vines. The heat of her angry breaths made his insides strain in his want to drink it, feel it, appease it. It sent him teetering into an aroused state he couldn't fathom, much less understand. Eyeing her in silence, he tugged at his tie, stripping it from his neck, breathing harshly.

"I'd say that went well."

She tilted her head, her eyes fierce, something there marking him as loathsome. "She didn't believe us for a moment, that we…" She turned away as if disgusted. "She didn't buy it."

He narrowed his eyes—watching the tantalizing rise and fall of her chest. How would they feel to the touch? Soft. Yes, God, soft and small. Perky? Yes, that, too. His mouth watered. "Whether she believes it or not is of no consequence now."

Her eyes flashed a glittery warning. "You wanted to make her jealous."

"Jealous," he repeated, puzzled by the accusation. "Is that what you believe?"

She shoved her hair back from her forehead. "Yes, it is. And I'm sorry I disappointed, Marcos."

His blood raged hot and wild. He'd never seen her like this. Almost out of control, begging for…something he wanted to give her. Suddenly he'd give anything to hear her utter his name in that same haughty, do-me tone. He'd do anything to just…bury this ache inside her.

"I look at her and feel nothing—not even anger anymore. I didn't want her jealousy, but I didn't want her insinuating herself into my bed either."

"Because you want her there. Otherwise you wouldn't need me standing between you!"

He grabbed her arms and jerked hard, spurred by every ounce of pent-up desire in him, harbored for too long. "Listen to you!" She slammed against him with a gasp. Her eyes flamed in indignation and his body roared to life, singed by her lushness, her mouth so close. "There's only one woman I want in my bed—one. And I've wanted her for a long, long time."

"Then go get her!"

He backed her toward the bedroom. "Oh, I will—and I'll have her right where I want her." He dragged her closer and pulled her dress beneath her breasts and her scent, sweet and warm, washed through his senses. He seized a nipple with two fingers and pushed her breast up to his mouth and sucked.

He paused briefly to say, "The thought of you has me tied into knots. I want to taste you. For you to give me your lips, feel my body in yours. I want you coming with my name on your lips, coming over and over, with me."

She caught his head and moaned. He could see the needs, the emotions, rising in her and darkening her eyes to storms. His hands caught her wrists and pinned them over her head and tightened. "Share my bed."

"Marcos…"

A throbbing sensation pulsed through him, aching in his erection, his chest, his head. His voice grew hard, fierce as his cheek pressed against hers and he murmured in her ear. "I won't beg, not even for you, I won't ask again, Virginia. I have a craving for you…it's running wild and out of control. You share this craving. You crave me, you crave me so much you tremble with the force of it. Don't deny us. Don't deny me."

His breathing was ragged, hers wild. The gleam of defiance died out in her eyes as she gazed at his lips. He groaned and pulled her head to his as he swept down. His kiss was bred by passion, rampant with lust. The raging desire threatened to consume his mind, his sanity. He was undone by her kiss, her taste. His mind raced, his thirst for her sweeping through him. Her response was wholehearted, fiery, and it almost sent him to his knees. Her mouth sipped, her hands took what he wanted to give her. He called upon restraint but there was only passion here. Over and over he thought of being gentle, over and over her answer was to intensify, demand more.

He grabbed her and thrust her onto the bed, bouncing, and he was ripping at his shirt.

She climbed to her knees, her hands on her dress, fumbling to unbutton.

He whipped his shirt off, meeting her glimmering green gaze, stripping naked. "Do you want me?"

"Yes."

He unbuckled his belt and sent it slapping to the floor. "Lie back."

His heart thundered as he waited for her to, aware of the erection straining before her, listening to her sharp inhale. She backed away, her dress riding up to show her blue panties. And she was… There were no words. That lacy blue stuff looked delicious on her.… He wanted to use his lips to pry it off, his teeth… No, he couldn't wait; he needed to feel her skin.

He fell on her and trapped her under him, yanking her arms up, his pelvis arching into her. "You'll take what I can give you, all of it, *amor.*"

"Yes."

She struggled against him, but he tamed her with his mouth, pinning her with his weight, stretching out naked on top of her. He grabbed her hair and held her still, and it felt like silk between his fingers. "I'm going to love doing this with you."

She sighed and rubbed against him like a cat. "I'll pretend to like it."

Her voice was husky, full of longing, inviting him to do

things to her. He cupped the full globes of her lace-covered breasts, dragging his teeth across that delectable spot of skin, licking the curve between her neck and shoulder. "Oh, you will. I'll make sure you do." Her nipple puckered, and he pinched to draw it out even more. "This little nipple pretends very well."

She lay back, all skin and hair and woman, drawing him to her warmth. Her arms were around him, her hands on his back, kneading the bunched-up muscles. He shuddered. He could lose himself in those eyes, in that body, in her, and he demanded, "Say 'Marcos.' Whisper my name to me."

"Marcos."

She wasn't sure from what part of her had come this determination, this courage or this desperate want, she only knew she needed him. He annihilated her mind, her senses. She hadn't realized what she'd do, how she'd fight to be with this one man until she'd seen Marissa.

She hadn't yet finished saying his name, a word that echoed the passion roaring through her, and he was there already, growling "Virginia" and taking her mouth in a fierce kiss. A flock of butterflies exploded in her stomach when their lips met. Her head swam as the flames spread, his tongue thrusting precisely, strongly, fiercely inside, emotion hissing through her, weakening her, overwhelming her.

Growling, he deepened the kiss as he tugged the bow loose at her hip, and she felt the fabric of her dress unfurl until it opened and hung at her sides. "It's important your body becomes familiar with my touch. All of it. You want Marissa to believe us, don't you? If you want others to believe it you have to believe it yourself. Your body has to know to respond when I touch it."

A strangled sound echoed in the silence and in the back of her mind Virginia realized it came from her. He cupped one lace-encased breast. Oh, it was so wonderful. So bad. So everything. She'd stop him in a minute…in one more minute…no, she'd not stop him, not tonight, maybe not ever.

Utterly possessing her lips, he slid his free palm down the flatness of her stomach and below. "It's important I know your curves…the texture of your skin…"

She could feel every sinew of his muscles against her. His fingers…sliding downward. Deep, forgotten places inside her clenched in waiting for his touch. Opening her mouth, she flicked her tongue out to his. "Marcos."

"Here you are. Soaked."

His voice grew husky. Desire trembled there. His hand between her legs began to slide under her panties. She arched involuntarily when he feathered a finger across the soft, damp spot at the juncture of her thighs. Every pink, throbbing part of her pinged at his touch. She moaned in her throat and sank back deeper into the bed as he caressed more deliberately.

She'd never known a touch could feel like fire, spread through her until every inch throbbed and burned. Involuntarily she moved her hips, filling his palm with the dewy softness between her legs.

"Marcos…" It was a plea, and it carried in it the fright she experienced in what he made her feel.

"Shh." His lips grazed her temple. "Open up to me." His free hand tugged at her bra and bared her left breast to him. Her disbelieving gaze captured the instant the rosy peak of her nipple disappeared between his lips. A thrilling jolt rushed through her as the moist heat of his mouth enveloped her. Her head fell back on a moan.

Instinctively she reached up to cup the back of his head, cradling him with the same gentle care he used to suckle her breast. He groaned profoundly in his throat and continued to fondle her with his mouth, lips nipping, tongue swirling, mouth suckling.

His hand moved lightly, expertly, his fingers unerringly

fondling her through her panties. Hot little shivers rushed through her.

One long finger began to stroke her dampness. Open her with little prods of the tip.

She squirmed in shock, a little in agony, seeking ease for the burn growing inside her. "I hurt." Blindly, her parted mouth sought more of the warmth of his lips. He penetrated her. With his tongue. His finger. She arched and cried out, shocked by the sensation. An explosion of colors erupted behind her eyelids. His mouth melded to hers harder. Skin, heat, ecstasy.

Her skin felt damp while every cell in her body felt hot and tingly. With a low growl, he delved a hand into her hair and pulled her head back, moving his mouth up her neck. It was damp and velvety on her flesh, licking as though her skin were his only sustenance. In her ear he rasped, "I'm filling you."

"Yes." Against his throat.

"You crave me to fill you." His finger was thrusting, possessing—his body incredibly hard against hers. "You need me to take away the hurt."

Pleasure ripped through her, and her back arched helplessly as she moaned. "You make me reckless, Marcos, you make me…"

"Burn." He opened his mouth. Giving her the mist of his breath. "I can't believe how ready you are. How slick. Are you pretending? Are you, *amor?*"

"No."

He gave her his tongue. She could hear the soaked sounds his touch caused and felt embarrassed and aroused all at once. "Shh. Take my finger," he huskily murmured, the graze of that finger so bare and fleeting across her entry she mewled with a protest to take it in again. "Soon I'll give you two. Do you want two?"

"No," she lied. Her body ruled now, screamed, shivered against his.

"Hmm." He inserted the first, then the second deeply. "I'll pretend that was a yes."

Her thoughts scattered. "Marcos, please…"

"My God, you're responsive." His hands continued to work their magic as he looked down on her. "You were jealous for me."

The burn intensified. The clench in her womb unbearable. "Yes," she breathed, closing her eyes.

His groan sounded like a growl. "I like that."

"Marcos."

He was watching her, the effects of what he did to her. Every time she gasped, or let go a little moan, his face tightened with emotion—and alternately, something clenched tightly in her. She'd never known the extent of her passion, was surprised at how shamelessly she took pleasure from him.

Gently, he pried her fingers away from his neck and brought her hand between their bodies. "Touch me."

"Where? Where do I…"

"Here." He shifted over her. The sheets slid well below his hips and their every inch, shoulder to hips, became perfectly aligned. The very hardest part of him pushed against her hand. "Feel me," he strained out. "Feel how I want you. This isn't for her, Virginia, this is for you."

He ground his hips against hers unapologetically. When she let go, his rigid length grazed her moistness through her panties. They groaned at the contact. He pressed closer, ground himself harder, wide and long against her. She wanted to die.

By the erratic heaves of his chest, Virginia suspected even though he was larger and more powerful, he was as defenseless to their chemistry as she was. Under her fingers, his skin was warm and slightly damp. Shyly, she continued to explore him, sifting her fingers through the dark hair at his nape, amazed at the soft texture.

His hands covered her breasts. The calluses on his palms were palpable through the lace, and her breast swelled ripely under his kneading.

Turning her cheek into the pillow, she let her eyes drift shut as she fought the intimacy of it all, the swelling tenderness that washed over her as he touched her. It was difficult to imagine that he was not her lover and she wasn't entirely, completely, indisputably his.

Burying his face between her breasts, he gnawed at the tiny bow at the center of her bra. She felt the unmistakable graze of his teeth on her skin. He used them to scrape the top swell of her breast and a very startling whimper escaped her.

His mouth shifted to the peak, pointy and obvious under the fabric, and he licked her. The hot dampness of his tongue seeped into her skin. She shuddered. A thrilling heat fanned out from her center.

He reached around her and unhooked her bra. When he peeled it off her, she instinctively covered herself with her palms.

"I want to see." He pried her hands away and placed them on his shoulders. His dark, heavy-lidded eyes regarded each of her breasts with interest. His breath fanned across one exposed nipple. "So pretty."

She drew in a ragged breath as he brushed the little bud with the pad of his thumb. It puckered under his finger. If possible, his eyes darkened even more. "Do you want my mouth here?"

"I d-don't know."

He swiped his tongue across the tip. "Yes, you do." He closed his eyes and nuzzled her with his nose. "Do you want my mouth here?"

"Yes."

He licked gently. "Like that."

"Yes."

He grazed with his teeth. "Or like that."

She squeezed his shoulders, staring to shiver. "B-both."

He nibbled using his lips then drew her fully into his mouth. "Hmm. Like a raspberry."

Her eyes shut tight. The sensation of being devoured entirely by his mouth had her melting.

Could he say something wrong, please? Could he not lick her…like that? Could his hands be smaller, less thorough, less hot, less knowing?

Turning to suckle her other breast, he delved one hand between her legs and slipped into her panties. "I want my mouth here, too," he murmured, searching her pliant folds with strong, deft fingers.

She gasped and thrashed her head, seized by a mix of shame and pleasure as he unerringly found, opened, invaded that most intimate part of her. "N-no…no mouth there."

"But I can touch?"

Quivering and warm, she sensed him watching her as he gently eased one finger into that moist, swollen place that craved him.

She gulped back an enormous clog of emotion. "Yes."

"*Chiquita.*" It was a reverent whisper, full of wonder as he stretched her. "*Chiquita mia.*"

She arched, shamelessly offering herself. As he continued his foray inside her, a marvelous pressure gathered at her core.

His nostrils flared. "One minute," he rasped as he searched under her dress for the silken string of her panties. She was weightless on the bed when he tugged them off her legs. "And I put us both out of our misery."

His chest gleamed bare when he leaned over her, his shoulders bunched with tension as he grasped her calves.

He stared into her eyes, his expression tight as he guided her legs around his hips. "Hold on to me. Don't let me go."

The way he asked to be held made her think she'd never let him go, she'd make him love her, she'd hold on to him.

He pulled her to his hips and she felt him, hot and thick and rigid, pressing into where she was pliant and damp. A wildness raged inside her when he ducked his head to suckle a breast—suckle hard the instant he pushed in. She bucked up to receive him, urging him in with her hands and legs.

They moaned in unison when he entered, their breaths mingling as he angled his head to hers, their lips so close that all he had to do was bend his head an inch to capture her mouth and the whimper that followed when he was fully inside her.

"Yes," he growled.

"Yes," she breathed.

A fullness took her, bringing the discomfort of being stretched more than she could bear, and then he was moving inside her and the unease transformed to pleasure. Waves and waves of pleasure.

And in that instant she loved what he did to her, how he brought her every cell and atom to life, how he offered her ease. Ease for this wanting.

She'd longed for that ease more than anything.

As he moved in her, touched and kissed her, she gave encouraging sounds that seemed to tear out from within her—and he continued. Taking. Giving. Expertly loving her.

Braced up above her, his arms rippled with tension, his throat strained, his face was raw with the semblance of pleasure. All were memorized in her mind.

Vaguely, in her blanked, blissful state, she knew sex would never again be like this. Would a man ever live up to this one?

A sound that was purely male vibrated against her ear as he placed his mouth there to whisper, "Come for me."

Moving deftly, he pushed her higher and higher, murmuring carnal, unintelligible words in Spanish that melted her bones like the silk and steel thrusts of his body. *Mia. Suave. Hermosa. Mia. Mia. Mia.*

All Virginia could say was "Marcos." In a plea, a murmur, a moan. *Marcos.* Over and over again. *Marcos* as he increased his pace, driving faster, more desperately into her. Vaguely she felt the warmth of him spill inside her, the convulsions that racked his powerful body as ecstasy tore through them both, the pleasure consuming, making him yell, making her scream, scream "Marcos."

"Marcos" as he kissed her breasts, her lips, her neck. "Marcos" as the pressure spread. "Marcos" as she shattered.

Seven

Darkness: it was hard to leave it. But a strong, familiar scent wafted into her nostrils. Tempting. Tantalizing. Beckoning her awake. Coffee. Yes. Strong and rich and ready. Virginia stirred on the bed. She stretched her arms first, then her legs, sighing when it hurt pleasantly to do both.

"...in an hour...yes...we'll be there..."

Virginia bolted upright on the bed when she recognized that particularly deep baritone voice. Her head swam. *Lips tugging at her nipples, fingers pinching, touching, pleasuring...whispers...* A throb started between her legs. She squeezed her eyes shut and swung her feet until her toes touched the carpeted floor. *Calm down.* She would not, could not, panic.

Sunlight glowed in the living room, making her squint as she entered. He stood by the window in his shirt and slacks. His raven-black hair looked damp from a recent bath. He held one arm stretched above his head, his tan hand braced on the windowsill. His was a solid presence in the room.

Sturdy as an ox, that was the way he looked. That was the way he was.

"Good morning," she muttered.

He turned, smiled.

She set her coffee on a small round table beside the desk and lowered herself to a chair, Marcos coming forward and kissing her forehead.

"Did you order the entire kitchen contents up here?" she whispered.

He stroked her cheek. "I wanted to be sure I ordered what you liked."

A blush was spreading up her neck because she remembered cuddling against him after she'd gone on and on saying *please*. God, no.

His eyes were full of knowledge, of satisfaction of having loved his lover well and hard for a night. Her skin pebbled with goose bumps as she realized he was remembering everything they'd done through the night: the kissing, the laughing, the kissing, the eating cheese and grapes on the carpet, the kissing.

They had made love until Virginia thought she'd pass out from bliss.

And hours before waking up, when she had cuddled in and draped one leg across his hips, he had made slow, lazy love to her again, and whispered words to her in Spanish she could only dream of finding the meaning of.

He lifted her chin, studying her. "Did I hurt you last night?"

With a small smile, she tugged on the collar of her pajama top and showed him his bite. His forehead furrowed.

"That has to be painful."

"Only in the most pleasurable way."

Settling down, she took a healthy sip of coffee, then set the cup back down. "What?" she pressed.

He was looking at her strangely.

Send For
2 FREE BOOKS
Today!

I accept your offer!

Please send me two free Silhouette Desire® novels and two mystery gifts (gifts worth about $10). I understand that these books are completely free—even the shipping and handling will be paid—and I am under no obligation to purchase anything, ever, as explained on the back of this card.

About how many NEW paperback fiction books have you purchased in the past 3 months?

❑ 0-2
E7WH

❑ 3-6
E7WT

❑ 7 or more
E7W5

225/326 SDL

Please Print

FIRST NAME

LAST NAME

ADDRESS

APT.#   CITY

STATE/PROV.   ZIP/POSTAL CODE

Visit us online at
www.ReaderService.com

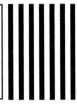

NO POSTAGE
NECESSARY
IF MAILED
IN THE
UNITED STATES

BUSINESS REPLY MAIL
FIRST-CLASS MAIL   PERMIT NO. 717   BUFFALO, NY

POSTAGE WILL BE PAID BY ADDRESSEE

THE READER SERVICE
PO BOX 1867
BUFFALO NY 14240-9952

"What?"

"You begged me to take you last night."

"And?"

"And I liked it."

Her stomach muscles contracted. Suddenly her lips felt puffy and sensitive as she remembered just how thoroughly he'd kissed her. "Marcos, this will be very complicated in Chicago."

"It doesn't have to be."

A thousand butterflies fluttered in her chest. "You expect we can keep this up?"

"We touched. We made love four times in one night. Do you expect we can stop by Monday?"

They'd touched. His tanned, long hands had been somewhere in her body, and hers had been somewhere in his. She couldn't bear to remember. "What do you…suggest?"

"Nobody has to know about us. And my suggestion is to continue."

Her body trembled. Little places zinged and pinged as though reminding her just, exactly, where his hands had been. "Continue."

He leaned against the window and his hand slowly fisted high up on the windowsill. "I swear I've never seen anything lovelier than you, naked. Your breasts."

She closed her eyes, sucking in a breath, willing herself not to remember what he'd done there. How he'd squeezed or cradled or…

"Marcos…"

"You cried out my name when I was inside you."

Oh, God. Yes, she had, yes, she had. Had she no honor? No pride when it came to him? No digni—

"I couldn't sleep for wanting to take you again." He smiled sadly. "You kept cuddling against me and I kept growing hard. I had to…shower."

Wrapping her arms around her shaking frame, she asked, "Do you want to?"

"To what?"

"Make love to me again."

And he said…

"Yes."

Her stomach exploded. He wanted her. Still. More than yesterday? Marcos still wanted her. But they couldn't continue in Chicago. They couldn't.

His arm fell at his side as he spun around and pinned her with a smile. "Eat up, though. We're going sightseeing."

She set down her coffee mug before she spilled it all over herself. "Really?"

"Of course. Really. We're flying over the city on a chopper first. Then we'll lunch downtown."

"A chopper."

"Are you concerned?"

"Actually, no. Excited."

She dug into the eggs, the waffles and the tea.

Marcos was piling his plate as though he hadn't been fed since his toddler years. "Would you like a tour of Allende," he asked casually.

Allende. She grinned. "I thought you'd never ask."

It occurred to her she had never imagined she could ever have one of these mornings with Marcos. Such a lavish, elegant hotel suite and such a clear, sunny day outside, a beautiful morning. Like husband and wife. Talking. Smiling. Laughing as they enjoyed breakfast. But they were boss and assistant, embarking on what had to be wrong. The air around them was charged with sexual tension. Really, it could very well be lightning in there.

"Did she…agree to your bid?" Virginia asked, breaking the silence. This watching him eat was a little too stimulating to her mind.

He popped a grape into his mouth. "She will."

"She didn't seem interested in even discussing business."

"It's a game." His eyes skewered her to her seat. "She wants me to demand Allende and I won't."

"So you'll play this for the entire week."

"Not likely." He spread cream cheese atop his bagel. "I'll leave with an offer and let her think it over."

Were he any other man, Virginia was sure a woman like Marissa could handle him. But he was Marcos. Nobody could think straight with him near and he was as manageable as a wild stallion to a child. "If she rejects your offer?"

He diverted his attention from his tower of gluttony and selected a newspaper among the three folded ones, calmly saying, "She's not getting a better one, trust me."

He yanked open *El Norte*. "What angered you? Yesterday?"

The cup paused halfway to her lips then clattered back down on the plate. "I heard you…discussing me. I've always found that annoying."

Slowly he folded the paper and set it aside. The intense stare he leveled on her made her squirm. Those gypsy eyes, they did magic in her. Black magic.

"You're blushing."

"I'm not."

But her face felt hot and so did other parts of her.

His jaw tightened and a muscle in his cheek flexed. "Is it the attention? You do not like this?"

She drew in a deep breath because unfortunately there was no brown bag she could cover her face with. She had to pretend he was hallucinating. "It's the whispering behind my back."

"You cannot control what people whisper." He popped a piece of his bagel into his mouth and then picked up the paper again.

"You are wrong." How could he think that? "You can

control your actions. You can give them no cause to...to whisper."

"You'd let gossip hurt you, Virginia?"

His voice was full of such tenderness she actually felt it like a stroke. "You've never been hurt by words before?"

Once again, the paper was lowered. This time his eyes burned holes through her. "I said words to my father. I'll bet my fortune that yes, they hurt."

Something distressed her. His gaze. His tone. "You wish you took them back?"

He considered with a frown. "No. I wish he'd have taken them for what they were. The words of a wounded boy determined to break him."

She had never known Marcos to be cruel. But he could be dangerous. He was predator, and he had been wounded. "You could never make amends with him?"

His smile was pantherlike, almost carrying a hiss. "Because of her."

"Marcos," she said again after a moment, even more alarmed at the harsh set of his jaw and ominous slant of his eyebrows. "Marcos, why do you want to destroy the company? You could make amends with it. Save it, mend it."

"It would take too much effort." He waved her off with a hand, went back to the paper. "Eat up, *amor,* I'm eager to show you the city."

"You're eager to get back and have your way with me," she quipped.

He threw his head back and gave out a bark of laughter, his expression so beautiful her heart soared in her chest. "So we understand each other, then."

He couldn't tear his eyes away from her.

She was the same woman he'd wanted for so long, and yet she had become someone else. A sexy woman who was comfortable in his presence, smiling, laughing, open to speaking her mind.

Eyes sparkling as the helicopter touched the ground, Virginia pulled his headphones down to his neck. "That's Allende?" she yelled through the rotor noise.

He glanced out the window, squeezing her fingers with his. Impossible, but her excitement was rubbing off on him. "That's it, yes."

Once they climbed out of the helicopter, Marcos surveyed the vast industrial building that sat on two hundred acres of land. It was smaller than he remembered it—but then he'd been so much younger.

The sun blazed atop their heads. Virginia's raven mane gleamed. And in that moment Marcos didn't see how aged the building appeared, or notice the grease on all the trucks and carriers that were parked in endless rows across the parking lot. He saw his father and himself, discussing the delivery schedule. A strange heaviness settled in his chest, weighing him down.

"Are we going in?"

Pulled from his thoughts, he looked at his assistant. How she managed to stand there—sexy and innocent—while he felt so unsettled was beyond him.

Bracing himself for whatever greeted him inside, he led her toward the double glass doors beneath a metal sign that read *Transportes Allende*.

Within minutes the two guards unlocked the door and ushered them in. Marcos and Virginia were free to roam the old wide halls. An attractive blush tinted her cheeks as she eagerly drank in her surroundings.

There was nothing to say about the structure, except that it was bare bones, obsolete and old. *Horrible.*

New installations were a must. A more recent fleet of carriers to strengthen their position as a link to the U.S. market. New—

"This is terribly spacious," she said, leaning a hand on a red brick wall that served as a room division.

Marcos reined himself back. What in *the hell* had he been thinking?

He didn't want to restore the company to its former glory; he wanted it gone.

He frowned darkly while Virginia swayed her hips and went peeking from room to room. All were vacated for the morning under Marcos's instructions. An encounter with Marissa was the last thing he'd wanted today—and thankfully she was smart enough to have obliged.

Virginia tucked her hair behind her ear, her forehead creasing as she peered up at the rafters on the ceiling.

Rather than notice the paint was peeling off the walls and making a list of fixing that—Miss Hollis was probably already cataloguing that for him, in any case—Marcos focused on her reactions.

Something warm and fuzzy stirred in him. Virginia would be a pitiful poker player. Her expressions were too untrained for intrigue—and her father's past had given her a loathing for the game.

"My first office," he said then, without tone.

She spun around in the doorway as he spoke, wide-eyed. "This one? With the view of the front gate?"

He followed her into the small space and tried to see it through her eyes, old and dirty and cluttered, but then it just appeared like what it was: a promising place in need of some attention.

Marcos could've kicked himself for mentally volunteering to give it some TLC. No. Hell, no.

He wouldn't.

All he wanted was to eliminate it, like wiping out his past in one fell swoop. Swoosh. Gone. Presto!

But judging by the interest that swam in Virginia's eyes,

she approved of the place, too. "It fits you somehow," she said. "Rough around the edges."

They shared a smile.

The fuzzy feeling inside him grew to incredible proportions.

"How many transport units does it have?" she asked. "Approximately?"

He watched her sail to the window. His eyes tracked her progress for a moment and then he followed her.

She was peering through the blinds, scanning the vast loading area, when he came up behind her.

He buried his face in the side of her neck and enveloped her in his arms, biting back a groan. "There are two thousand and forty cargo carriers—plus hundreds of smaller units for simpler deliveries."

She smelled of a soft, powdery fragrance, her hair scented with his travel shampoo. The combination flew up to his head like an aphrodisiac.

He'd never imagined the days they spent together would be like this. Lust and desire constantly had him on edge, true, but there was also the delightful peace and pleasure of her company.

Gently, he guided her around to face him. "As soon as we land in Chicago, I will have the funds transferred to your personal account. I want those men out of your and your father's lives so you can be at peace. Agreed?"

A shadow descended, veiling her eyes. Inch by inch, her smile disappeared.

He cupped her face between his palms. "Something wrong with that?"

Clearly something was. She averted her gaze and gnawed on her lower lip. "Thank you, no, it's all fine. That's our arrangement, right?"

Pretend, she didn't say. But his mind supplied it.

When Marcos did not deny this, Virginia lowered her

face and drew away, suddenly looking very young and very vulnerable. She hugged herself tight. "I'd forgotten I'm being paid for this, that my father's bad habits brought me here."

Marcos knew that a woman like her didn't easily fall into a man's bed. Was she regretting that she had? Or only the circumstances that had brought her there?

A host of male instincts assailed him, urging him to embrace her, take her, appease her, seize the instinctive role of a man and protect her.

With a surge of dominant power, he grasped her shoulders and gave a gentle clench. "You're worried he won't stop gambling—that this will only be a temporary relief from your problem."

She nodded. "I am."

Virginia had been calling her father every day. His insides wrenched in protest at the knowledge of her suffering because of a reckless old man on a suicide mission. "How long since your father had a real job?" They strolled back into the hall, side by side.

"Since Mother died. Several years ago."

They came into the last office—his father's old office. Virginia probably didn't know it had been his because of its ample size, or maybe she suspected, Marcos didn't know. All he knew was that he couldn't bear to look around but at the same time couldn't leave it.

He crossed the wood floor, now covered with a shaggy white rug, and touched the window as he gazed outside. "He's been like this ever since? Your father?"

"It's gotten out of control recently."

Circling around the desk, he stroked the blunt edge with his fingers—he used to sit there and listen to his father talk on the phone. Thoughtfully, he asked, "Has he tried to even get a job?"

"He did. He's tried, but of course he's found nothing. At

least that's what he says, but I suspect his pride won't let him accept the kinds of jobs that have been offered to him."

He frowned. "Sometimes you have to take what you can get."

"I agree." She toed the plush ends of the rug with the tip of her high heels. "I just feel he was hoping for someone to give him a chance at what he used to do. He was a good manager except he spoiled his chance."

Second chances, Marcos thought. People spoke of them all the time, but in reality nobody offered them.

His father hadn't offered it to him.

Nor had he offered one to his father.

Gradually, he allowed his surroundings to filter into his mind. A snapshot of Marissa beside the dormant computer. Frilly female things atop the desk. And he realized with a sinking heart that Marissa had taken possession of his father's office.

There was no picture of the old man who'd raised him. The soccer posters—vintage ones that his old man had collected— were no longer on the walls. She'd taken everything, that heartless witch. *Everything!*

"This is your father's office?" Virginia watched him, and the pity in her eyes made him desperate to eliminate it.

"Not anymore." He smiled tightly, snatching up her hand. "Come on, let's go. The office staff is coming in later."

He escorted her outside. Thinking of how it was too late for his father and him—but maybe not for hers. Marcos's old man had not been a gambler, but his quest for a woman had trampled his own son.

It seemed unfair a child should sacrifice their happiness for a parent. Marcos had not been willing.

He'd *never* accept as a stepmother a woman who'd months before been his lover, *never* accept as a stepmother a woman who was so obviously playing his father for a fool. After numerous heated arguments where Carlos Allende refused to admit his son's view as true, Marcos had packed his bags and left. But Virginia?

When her father fell into that dark gambling pit once more, what was this generous, loyal creature going to do? And what would he be willing to do to help her?

She loved Mexico.

There was something deliciously decadent about the time they spent during the following days poking around little shops, eating in restaurants, walking the city.

This afternoon, as Virginia's heels hit the marbled floors of the awe-inspiring MARCO museum, she drew in a deep, reverent breath. This was a luxury she'd never allowed herself before. She'd rarely allowed herself outings to relax or to stimulate the mind; she'd always been so consumed by worry.

Now she wove through the paintings on exhibit, feeling Marcos's presence next to her, and felt like she'd stepped into an alternate reality.

Every painting that caught her eye, every sculpture she viewed with the eyes of a woman who had suddenly acquired sight. And hearing. And touch. The colors were vibrant, and the themes were all passionate. Even death seemed passionate.

At night, Marcos took her out to eat in a small café just blocks away from the city plaza. After salad, tacos and fries, they walked arm-in-arm through the throng of people.

She'd never felt so safe.

She was in a dangerous city, surrounded by a language she did not understand and among unique, intriguing people, and she felt utterly safe. Her world felt so distant. Her father's debts, the threats, the fact that things could get worse. Nothing mattered when these long, sinewy, rock-hard arms were around her.

She felt, for the first time in her life, protected. *Secure*.

During their ride back to the hotel, she caught Marcos watching her with those eyes and that knowing smile, and a sneaky little voice whispered to her. It accompanied them to their rooms, nestling somewhere deep inside her.

This is as real as real gets, Virginia Hollis. Can you make him see it?

No, she doubted that she could. He viewed the world with the eyes of a man. While she, with those of a woman.

As she struggled to tame her welling emotions, Marcos grasped her chin between his thumb and forefinger and tipped her head back. "Who does he gamble with? Do you know?"

It took a moment for her to grasp his train of thought. She shook her head. "I don't know."

Marcos hadn't dropped the subject of her father for days. It was as though he were intent on avoiding the topic of his own parent and was focusing instead on fixing the troubles of hers.

Shrugging off his shirt, his eyes held hers in the lamplight, his voice a mellow rumble. "You said his gambling put you in this position. In that bed right behind you. My bed. Did you mean it?"

She considered the question at length, and though she'd needed to save her father no matter what, she also softly admitted, as she pulled off her short-sleeved sweater, "I think I brought myself here."

She tossed her sweater aside, then her bra. Even in the flickering shadows, she caught the tightening flex of his jaw and throat. That her nakedness affected him made her smile and move close to him. Her palms hit the smooth velvet of his chest and her fingers rubbed upward. "What do you say about that, Mr. Allende?" she whispered.

With slow deliberation, he turned his head toward hers. As his fingers ventured in a languorous caress up her back, his mouth grazed her cheek and his sweet, hot breath coasted across her skin. "I say you're the sexiest little thing I've ever seen. Miss Hollis. And I want you to promise me—whatever happens between us, you're coming to me if your father's ever again in trouble."

"No, Marcos."

"Yes. You are. I'd make you give me your word you'll not pay debts that aren't yours, but I know that'd be unfair to ask of you. You feel responsible for him, I respect that. Now please understand I feel responsible for you."

Her toes curled at the proprietary gleam in his eyes. "But you're not."

"You're my employee."

"You have thousands of employees."

His knuckles caressed her nipples, and her body flared to life at the touch. "But only one who's been my lover."

The words lingered in the air for a heated moment. She was ready to give up. Just wanted to kiss. Could almost hear the seconds ticking as their time together ran out.

"No contest?" he queried then, sensing his victory.

She yielded, shaking her head, wrapping her arms around him. "None."

By the time their lips touched, she was holding her breath, parting her lips for his smiling mouth to take. He seized them softly and began to entice and torment her with nips and nibbles and gentle little suckles she felt down to the soles of her feet.

When he lowered her to the bed, his mouth became more demanding, spreading fire through her veins. And as his tongue forayed hard and hot inside her, one hand traveled up her ribcage to knead one waiting, throbbing breast with long, skillful fingers. *"Chiquita."*

He scraped his whiskers across her chin, and she sighed.

She was his lover for a week.

She was nothing more and she would never be more.

Braced up on one arm, he used his free hand to unbuckle her slacks. He pulled the zipper low and pulled them off her. His thumb touched the elastic of her panties and made slow, sinuous circles before he eased it down.

Lover for a week. That's all.

Discarding her panties, he urged her down on the bed and rained haphazard, unexpected kisses across her torso. On her shoulder, her tummy, then feasted on the tip of one breast. Virginia dropped her hand and absently caressed the back of his satiny black head as it moved, imagining what it would be like to suckle a baby. Their baby.

She'd always wanted a family.

Virginia, lover for a week!

As he kissed a path down her belly, it struck her with a sweet wrenching pain that she had never sensed her dream of a family so far out of reach. At first the desire had been tucked aside to help her father resurface from his grief. Now it had come to the forefront of her mind and it mocked her.

Because she had become lover to this man.

This enthralling black-haired Spaniard.

And every man in her future would always be compared in her mind to Marcos Allende. Every bed she slept in would not be this one. And she dreaded, doubted there would be a man in this world to kiss her the way he did. Touch her like this, just like *this*.

Realizing his mouth was approaching somewhere dangerous, she squirmed under him. "If you knew what I was thinking," she spoke up at the ceiling, "you'd leave the room."

He lifted his head and met her gaze, his voice frighteningly solemn. "Don't give me your heart, Virginia."

Oh, God. She squeezed her eyes shut. *Don't fall in love with him, don't fall in love with him,* don't fall in love with him. She scoffed, yanked her arm free as she sat up. "What? You think you're all that and then some? That I cannot resist you? I'll have you know…my heart…was not part of our bargain. You're the boss and I'm the…employee and this is…an arrangement."

One callused palm ran up and down the side of her leg. "And yet it's easy to forget who we are here, isn't it? Easy to get confused."

She frowned over the concern in his voice and grabbed his head, defiantly pulling his lips to hers.

Lovers. That was all.

This is as real as real gets, Virginia Hollis. Can you make him see it?

They came to understand each other. Too well, maybe. They talked, but not of the future. They talked, but not of themselves.

They pretended, as they'd agreed to do.

"Did you enjoy yourself this week?"

Riding to the airport in the back of the Mercedes, Virginia sat curled up against Marcos's side and laid her cheek on his shoulder. It was strange—how instinctively she sought this place, and how instinctively Marcos wrapped his arm around her shoulder to offer it to her.

She didn't care if she shouldn't do this, only knew within hours she wouldn't dare. So she did it now.

"It's been wonderful," she admitted and trailed off when he brushed his mouth across her temple and placed a soft, almost imperceptible kiss there. "Unexpected and…surreal and wonderful."

He held her so tight, so intimately, and whispered against her hair, "We should've done this before."

Going pensive at the note of lingering lust in his voice, Virginia played with the buttons on his shirt while Marcos checked his phone and made a call to the office. As he spoke into the receiver, she stole a glance at him.

His voice rumbled in her ear, and his arm around her

was absently moving up and down her bare arm. She'd been unable to keep from staring at him all week, and had been secretly delighted that most times he'd been checking up on her, too.

When he hung up, he gazed out the window at the passing car lights and said, "You'll wire yourself the money from my account and take care of your problem straight away. Promptly, tomorrow morning."

A command. As an authoritative man and, also, her boss.

"Understand?"

She hadn't noticed she'd flattened her hand on his chest until his own big one came to cover hers. She watched their fingers entwine. Lovers' fingers.

God, she'd done the most reckless thing. Look at her—draped all over her boss. Imagine if this ever got out? If people knew? Worse of all, her tummy was in a twist because she loathed for it to stop. And it had to—tonight. "Yes, I'll take care of it right away," she murmured, and on impulse took a good long whiff of his familiar scent.

"I've been thinking." Marcos turned her hand around for his inspection and his thumb began to slowly circle the center of her palm. "I'd like to offer your father a job."

"A job?"

"I figure if he realized he could be useful, he'd break the cycle of vice he seems to be stuck in."

She thought about it, still resting her cheek against his chest, feeling utterly contented and yet dreading tomorrow when that feeling could be replaced with unease. "Why?" she asked then.

He quirked an eyebrow, then narrowed his eyes. "Why what?"

She fingered the heavy cross at his throat. "Why... him?"

"Why not?"

She shrugged, but her heart began to flutter at the prospect. "Maybe he's just hopeless." As hopeless as she was. How would she bear Monday at the office? She was terribly in lust with the man. He was an extraordinary lover, made her feel so sexy and wild she wanted to take all kinds of risks with him, and now he offered her father this incredible lifeline?

"Maybe he is hopeless," Marcos agreed, chuckling.

But no, he was not hopeless, no one was. A smile appeared on her face. "Or maybe he will want one more chance." And maybe she could handle Monday after all.

She'd survived so far, had feigned not to want Marcos for days and weeks and months. Now she'd act as though nothing had happened. As though when he looked at her, her insides didn't leap with joy, and when he smiled at her, her stomach didn't quiver.

He smiled at her then, causing all kinds of happenings in her body, and stroked her cheek with his warm hand. "I've looked into him. He was a smart, dedicated man, and he could be one again."

Virginia contemplated his words, pleased that Marcos was smart enough to look past her father's mistakes and see the hardworking man underneath. And a plan formed in her mind. Her father had managed a large chain store so successfully that, if everything hadn't gone downhill after her mother's death, he'd be CEO by now.

"You know, Marcos," she said quietly, straightening on a burst of inspiration, "I think he might enjoy coming to Mexico."

Silence fell. The car swerved to the left and into the small airport driveway. Virginia remembered the look of grim solemnity in Marcos's face during their tour of Allende and she plunged on.

"He might even enjoy working at Allende," she said. She tossed the bait lightly, hoping to plant some kernel of doubt in him so he'd reconsider his decision regarding the company's future. But he went so still, she almost regretted it.

He stared at her with a calculating expression, then gazed out at the waiting jet. "Maybe."

Neither said another word, but when he pulled her close, ducked his head and kissed her, she fought not to feel a painful pang.

This was where they'd first kissed.

It only made sense it would be where they had their last.

Eight

She was tidying up his office the next morning when Marcos halted at the doorway. The sight of Virginia fiddling with the coffeemaker froze him, then heated up his blood.

As she poured a cup—black, as he liked it—the plain buttoned-up shirt she wore stretched across her breasts in a way that made watching feel like purgatory.

"Good morning."

She glanced up with a soft gasp. "Marcos—Mr. Allende." And there went her breasts again, swelling, pert and lovely as she took a little breath.

His heart thudded as they stared at each other, the words lingering in the air. *Mr. Allende.*

A word meant to erase everything that had happened in Monterrey, Mexico.

Having never expected she would make it this easy, he stepped inside and pulled the doors shut behind him. "Good morning, Miss Hollis."

He really could do this.

They'd pretended to be lovers before.

Now they would pretend they never had been.

Black coffee mug cradled against her chest, Virginia stared at him with the glazed wariness of a woman who feared that a man knew her secrets. "Can I get you anything, Mr. Allende?"

You.

He bit off the word, pulled off his jacket and tossed it onto the L-shaped sofa before he started for his desk. His head buzzed with thoughts of her. Her, smiling up at him from her place on his lap. She had an obsession with tidiness, and it showed. His office was pristine. She was a tidy little box, his Miss Hollis. Who would've known she'd be such a wanton in bed? So uninhibited? So sexy? So addictive?

"I hear you arrived home safely," he said, his groin stirring at the memory of their lovemaking. *Dammit, don't go there, man.*

"Yes, thank you." She flashed him one of those smiles that made his thoughts scramble. "And I caught up on my sleep a little."

"Excellent. Excellent."

His body clenched at her admission, for *he* hadn't had a wink of sleep since their return. He kept remembering her, innocent, cuddled up against him.

Diablos, he had never imagined he'd once again look at Monterrey with longing. Now he did.

He longed to be there with his assistant for another week where he knew exactly what to do with her.

Lips thinning in disgust at his own erotic thoughts, he took the coffee cup from her hands when she passed it to him and dismissed her with a wave. No use in delaying their parting. "That will be all. Thank you, Miss Hollis."

And with a painful wrench of mental muscle, he tore his eyes away and pushed her from his mind.

He had a business to take over.

* * *

Chicago felt different. The wind was the same, the noise, the traffic, and yet, it felt so different. She'd had to face Marcos at the office again today. Yesterday, their nonchalance toward each other had been so borderline pathetic she'd felt nauseated by the time she got home.

This morning, unable to stomach coffee, she made her way down the hall. The door to the extra bedroom where her father had been sleeping for the past couple of months was shut, and Virginia pressed her palm against it for a long moment, wondering if she should wake him. Let him know she was leaving for work. That everything had been taken care of and his debt absolved.

She decided she would call later instead and carried her small black duffel bag outside where the taxi waited, remembering Marcos's offer to give her father a job.

It had been easy then, to accept anything he'd wanted to give her. They'd been…involved. Now, Marcos Allende could calmly forget about it, as he'd forgotten the rest.

Worst of all was it hurt.

Even when she'd expected it.

As she stepped onto the amazingly busy Fintech nineteenth floor, Virginia hoped every employee would be in their usual flurries of movement and therefore too busy to notice she was fifteen minutes late.

But notice her they did.

The very moment her heels hit the carpet, a quiet spread throughout.

For the second day in a row, people glanced up from the copy machines. Behind their desks, heads lifted. The fact that everyone, everyone in the vast open space, knew and had probably discussed the fact that she had spent a week with Marcos in Monterrey became brutally evident. Deep inside, where all her fears were kept in a tight little bundle, she heard something.

They say she's his lover...

Had someone spoken that? Was she putting words and thoughts into their mouths because of her own regrets?

Dragging in a calming breath, she crossed the sea of cubicles, then went down the art-packed hallway. At the far end, to the right of the massive carved doors that led to Marcos's office, three identical rosewood desks stood. She slid in behind hers. The savvy Mrs. Fuller, who'd been with Marcos "longer than his mother has," was quick to make her way around her own tidy work place and greet Virginia. "He's very strange today," the older woman said, wide-eyed. "He smiled at me and he said 'thank you.'"

The words didn't diminish the kernel of fear settled in the pit of Virginia's stomach. If she so much as stepped out of her boundaries this week and onward...if she was fool enough to even remind him of Mexico...she dared not think of who would be sitting behind her desk next week.

"Then the deal must be going in his favor." Virginia attempted a teasing smile as she turned to get settled.

Lindsay, a young redhead near Virginia's age who'd also become her friend, drew up next to Mrs. Fuller. Their expressions were those of genuine excitement. "How was Mexico?" the older woman asked as Virginia sank into her chair and gazed at the top of her desk. A picture of her mother. A fake orchid. Her yellow markers sticking out of a silver can.

"Was it hot? I hear it's sweltering this time of year," Mrs. Fuller insisted. Virginia hadn't seen the woman yesterday since they'd reached Fintech later than normal.

"Yes," Virginia said, having no other answer to give a woman who was known through the entire building as levelheaded and kind.

As Mrs. Fuller's concerned gray eyes bored into the top of Virginia's head, she wished she could have been spared this encounter with even more fervor than she'd wished to avoid her last one with the dentist.

"He's been gazing out the window all morning, and with so much to do, that is so unlike him," Lindsay confessed under her cinnamon-scented breath. "And he asked me where you were."

Virginia was spared having to reply when the phones began their usual music. Struck as though by lightning, both Lindsay and Mrs. Fuller were spurred to action. They jumped behind their desks and began tackling the calls.

Ignoring the telephone ringing equally obnoxiously on her desk, Virginia tucked the duffel into the nook under the computer. She would not, could not, think of his mood meaning anything. Their deal would be over soon, after the Fintech dinner, and they would forget Mexico. He had promised it would not affect her job.

Inspecting her drawers and taking out her personal notepad and the colored clips she'd bought in a burst of secretarial enthusiasm, Virginia felt her throat close at the sudden memory of her mother. That hopeful light always in her eyes. Her warm, caring smile. She had always had a saying to cheer Virginia up. Would she have one for Virginia today? One about there always being something better out there? Better than Marcos?

"Miss Hollis, I hear you were out with the boss?"

She started in surprise. Fredrick Mendez, one of the youngest accountants, had propped his hip onto the corner of her desk and was eyeing her with a combination of amusement and mock despair.

"For a week," she stressed as she straightened in her chair.

"That's too much, Miss Hollis. Too much time without you. So, did you bring me a key chain?"

"Did you ask for one?"

"All right, at least show us some pictures," Fredrick

insisted. But when Virginia's usual friendly smile just would not come, he fell to his knees and clutched a hand to his chest. "Oh, Virginia, thy eyes shalt truth reveal—"

"Am I running a circus here, Mendez?"

The deep, clear voice, but most of all, the distinguished accent, struck Virginia like a cannon blast.

Her eyes flew to locate the source. Inches away, exiting the conference room and on his way to her, Marcos Allende was a sight to behold. Power and sophistication oozed from his every pore. His stride was slow and confident, his expression perfectly composed. And his every step kicked up her heartbeat. Six of his top lawyers followed.

Upon realizing who'd spoken, Fredrick's pale complexion turned in the space of a second to a tomato-red. He jumped to his feet and smoothed a hand along his polka-dot tie. "No, sir. I was just welcoming Virginia back on our behalf."

"Our?" He said the word as though Fredrick had no right to include himself in something he hadn't been invited to.

Turning to where Virginia sat with perfect poise behind the desk, Marcos thrust his hands into his pockets and silently contemplated her. "Don't you have work to do other than hound Miss Hollis," he said softly, and there was no doubt whom he addressed.

Fredrick took off with a mumbled "Yes, sir."

Without removing his eyes from her, he also said, "Brief me on the new stipulations when they're in."

In unison, the lawyers expressed their agreement and dispersed.

Without the buffer of their presence, there was nothing to pry those jealous black eyes from hers, no shield from the scorching possessiveness flickering in their depths.

Suddenly breathless, Virginia wondered if the blouse she wore today might be too white, or a little sheer? If her skirt was too short, her hair too unruly, the silver hoop earrings inappropriate for Fintech?

Meanwhile Marcos was the epitome of the worldly businessman.

He filled his black Armani like it had been tailor-made for those broad, square shoulders, which tapered down to his lean waist and narrow hips.

God! She could not believe the dark, breathtaking creature before her was her lover from Mexico.

Suddenly, as their gazes held, their eyes screaming with something dark and sinful, Virginia was certain the entire room thought she had slept with him. *They say she's his lover...*

Please, God, let no one ever know.

"Marcos," she said, moderating her tone. "I'm sorry I'm late, but I—"

Hands planted on the desk, Marcos stretched his arms out and in a single fluid move leaned forward. As his face neared her, Virginia saw Mrs. Fuller's eyes turn to saucers, and Lindsay almost fell back in her chair.

When the tip of his nose almost touched hers, she could focus on nothing else but six feet three inches of Marcos Allende. He ducked his head.

"Do you remember our deal?"

The murmur couldn't have been heard by anyone else. But she felt as if the clock, the world, stopped.

The feel of his breath on her face sent a torrent of warmth through her singing veins. "Yes, of course, I remember."

He leaned back a bit, regarding her as though he expected the same illumination he seemed to have experienced to have struck her, too. "After-work hours were included, weren't they?"

She couldn't explain the thrill she experienced, this inspiring and overwhelming happiness. He was asking for more, more from her, and not until this moment when she had his full attention had she realized how thirsty she'd been for it. "They were. Why do you ask? Is it that you need some assistance?"

His smile, slow in reaching completion, was meltingly sexy. "I do."

They say she's his lover...

She was plunging into a bottomless pit where surely there was nothing but heartache, and still, her blood was thrilling in her veins. "I'm always happy to be of assistance."

He gazed directly at her—the intent in his eyes unmistakable. "Be certain you present yourself at my apartment this evening. There's much to do."

She flushed beet-red, and scribbled in a yellow Post-it, *Is this what I think it is?*

He read it and tucked the note into his jacket, not before stroking her thumb with his, and sent her a look of such emotion and longing she almost wept. "Six p.m. sharp, Miss Hollis. I'm afraid it's an all-nighter."

He'd already started for his office when she blurted, "I can handle all-nighters."

"Good. This one's particularly hard."

When the doors closed shut behind him, whispers erupted, and Mrs. Fuller jumped to her feet and raced toward her in a flurry of mortification.

"Virginia. Please don't tell me this is what I think it is."

Heart pumping irregularly, Virginia grabbed her notepad. "I'd better go. The sales projections start in a few minutes and Marcos will want my notes." Oh, God, they had seen and heard all that, hadn't they?

Virginia, like putty in his hands. Marcos, suggesting she go to his place to...to...behave wickedly.

But the woman caught her by the shoulders and clenched tight with her fists, her face stricken. "Oh, sweetie, please say it isn't so!"

"Mrs. Fuller," Virginia said in a placating voice, patting

one of her hands for good measure. "I don't know what you mean, but there is nothing going on here, *nothing!*"

"Yes, there is. I've seen the way you look at him. You're a sweet young girl, an innocent little lamb, and Marcos is…a wolf! He's emotionally detached and you can't possibly—"

Virginia turned her head to hide her blush only to catch half the office staring at them. But Lindsay was smiling in glee behind her desk and sticking her thumbs up as though Virginia had just won the lottery.

Lowering her voice to a whisper, Virginia confessed, "I can handle wolves. I can handle a pack of them, I promise you. And this is nothing like what you think."

"Vee. Sweet, sweet Vee." Mrs. Fuller's hands trembled when she framed her cheeks between them. "I adore Marcos like a son. He has been a kind boss to me, and when my poor Herbert died…" She sighed, then shook her perfectly coiffed head and got back on track. "But he is not the kind of man a woman like you needs. There hasn't been a single woman in his history he's kept around for more than a month. You'll end up with a broken heart and even lose your job."

That her last comment struck a nerve was a given.

"I'm not losing my job for anything." Virginia forced a smile to her face and much needed courage into her heart. She wanted him. She wanted him so bad she had to have him, would seduce and remind him. "He's my boss, and he wants me to assist him, and so I will. Please don't worry, Mrs. Fuller, or your heartburn will act up. I'll be fine. And be sure everyone, *everyone* knows there's nothing going on here."

But even as she stepped into the projection room, she couldn't help wondering how well they'd be able to hide it for as long as it lasted.

And what would happen to her when it was really, truly finished.

Nine

After the longest work day of his entire life, and one during which he'd gotten exasperatingly little work done, Marcos arrived home to find her waiting in his living room.

Of course. His assistants had his key code—why shouldn't she be here?

With the sun setting behind her, her feet tucked under her body on the couch, and a book spread open on her lap, Virginia Hollis was a welcoming sight.

When he stepped out of the elevator that opened into the penthouse, she came to her feet, her hands going to her hair—to her rich, curly black hair, which was deliciously tousled as though she'd been running her fingers through it all day.

He fisted his hands at his sides, his mouth going dry. Good God. She wore drawstring pants and a button-up shirt with little ice cream cones. The colorful, almost childish pattern was also stamped all across the pajama pants. And on her, that weathered, warm-looking thing was the sexiest garment he'd ever had the pleasure of gazing upon.

He hadn't intended to sleep with her. Or had he? He'd wanted to see her, damn it. And now he could hardly believe what she was so obviously offering to him.

When he finally spoke, his voice came out rougher than he'd anticipated. "Have a good day?"

She set her book on the side table. Nodded. Then, "You?"

God, this was so domestic he should be climbing back into the elevator right about now. And getting away from there as fast as he could.

Why didn't he?

Because his hands itched to touch her. His guts felt tight and he was hot and hard with wanting her. He'd wanted to drag her into his office today, feel his way up her little skirt, kiss that mouth until her lips were bright red. He couldn't stay away, had now determined he was a fool to.

She wanted him, too.

Removing his jacket, he draped it across the back of a chair, nodding, as well.

"I brought my notes," she said quickly. "Just in case."

He gazed into eyes that were green and bottomless, and slowly advanced. "Good. Notes are important," he offered in return, and because he had missed the enticing, arousing sight of her all day, he gruffly added, "What else did you bring me, Miss Hollis?"

The soft smile that appeared on her lips trembled. Her hands smoothed her pajamas all along her hips and his eyes greedily swept up and down the length of her. "I like that… thing you're wearing." More than that, he was warming up to the idea of tearing it off her and licking her like vanilla ice cream.

"Thank you." She signaled at his throat. "I—I like your tie."

He wrenched it off, tossed it aside, then closed the space

between them. "Come here," he said quietly, wrapping an arm around her waist and drawing her flat against his body. "Why are you so shy all of a sudden?"

She set her hands lightly on his shoulders, barely touching him. "I—I don't know. I shouldn't have slipped into my pajamas."

Lust whirled inside him. She had a way of staring at him with those big eyes, like he was something out of this world. And she felt soft and womanly against him, her scent teasing his lungs as he buried his face in her hair. "I've wanted this, Virginia. God, how I've wanted this."

As she tipped her head back to him, he covered her lips with his.

Employing every ounce of experience and coaxing power at his disposal, he began to feast on that little mouth, drink of her honey.

Hesitantly she dipped her tongue into his mouth and a pang of longing struck in his core at how sweet she tasted, how entirely she succumbed and fitted her body to his.

In his need, he didn't hear himself, the way his voice turned hoarse with longing as he spoke to her, cupping the back of her head gently. *"Delicioso...besame...dame tu boca..."*

She tasted of warmth and hunger, and responded like a woman who'd thought of him all day—wanted him all day.

Just as he had thought of ways of devouring her, too.

The kiss went, in the space of three seconds, from a hard quest to a need that left no room for finesse. While he took thirsty sips of her mouth, his hands went places, one to cup a plump buttock, the other to work on her shirt.

Her eager hands tugged his shirt out of the waistband of his pants and slipped inside, making him groan when her cool, dry palms caressed his chest up and down.

He imagined lifting her, wrapping her legs around him and taking her, and she jumped as though she were thinking the same thing, kissing him like no woman had ever kissed him before. She curled one shapely leg around him, and his hands went to his zipper.

"Damn." He halted, then set her slowly on her feet. Restless, as he drew back, he rubbed the straining muscles at the back of his neck.

They were breathing hard and loud.

Her hand flew up to cover her moist, glistening lips. "I... I'm sorry. I didn't mean to bite you."

That little bite had made him want to bite her back, in every place imaginable. Damn. He rubbed his face with both hands, his blood thrumming in his body. He'd undone three buttons of her pajama top, and the flesh of one breast threatened to pop out.

Marcos regarded the creamy flesh while an overwhelming urge to dip his fingers inside the cotton and weigh that globe in his hand made him curl his fingers into his palm.

"Marcos?"

He jerked his eyes away, stared at the top of her head. "I had a long day." *And I thought of nothing but this moment.*

He'd been out of his mind with jealousy at the sight of her flushed cheeks, that clown Mendez begging at her feet. How many men had stared at her, wanted her, like Marcos did?

Oblivious to the rampant storms of his thoughts, Virginia followed him down the hall and into the bedroom. He was a mass of craving and thirst and he'd never felt so perilously close to losing control before.

Crossing the length of the room, he braced a hand on the window and gazed out at the city. If she ever dared make a fool of him...if she ever dared so much as look at another man while she was with him...

"Marissa was after me for years."

A quiet settled, disturbed by the rustle of her clothes as she moved around. "I'm sorry."

Yes. Well.

So was he.

Such humiliation, the way she'd played him. "I didn't know my father wanted her," he said, unable to conceal the disgust in his voice, "until they were already...involved."

When he turned, she was standing by the bathroom door. She'd grabbed a brush and was pensively running it through her hair. The lights shone on the satin mass.

Entranced, Marcos watched the curls spring back into place after a pass, and he wanted to plunge his fingers through that hair and wrap it in his hands.

"Don't do that."

She stopped. It took him a moment to realize the hoarse, ragged plea had come from him. She lowered her arm.

"Do what?"

The cotton molded to her chest, rose and dipped in the most attractive places. Aware of how hard he was, how hot under his clothes, he feared his own instincts when she set the brush on the nightstand and directed her full attention on him.

"I'm not Marissa," she said, coming toward him.

He liked how candid she was. How she smiled with her eyes. How she walked. Talked. No, she was not Marissa.

Getting a grip of his thoughts, he shook his head. "I didn't say that." But it would be worse with her. If she ever hurt him. Deceived him. Betrayed him. He'd never trusted so fully, had never felt so many things at once.

"Marcos," she said softly. Her eyes were examining his stiff shoulders, the stony mask on his face, as she halted before him. He was shocked at the raw emotion shining in her eyes. Not only desire. But tenderness. Concern. Caring.

Caring that tugged at some little strings inside him.

Caring that begged him to care, too.

Damn.

She was his lover. He had a right to touch her, take her,

come with the pleasure of being inside her. It was all this was. Lust.

Lust lust lust.

"Never—" He could hardly speak as he lifted a hand to her silky, raven hair. She gasped at the touch, went very still.

"—ever—" he said gruffly, and tangled his fingers, fisted that lovely hair in his hand, using his knuckles to push her head up to where his lips waited "—lie to me."

He took her gasp, rubbed her lips farther apart, and traced their seam with his tongue. They were flavored with toothpaste and mint, and they were wet and hot. "Never lie to me with this mouth."

He licked into her, and she moaned. "I love this tongue, never lie to me with this tongue."

She inhaled a ragged breath and his tongue followed its path inside her, searching deep. In one instant her hands curled wantonly around his wrists, went higher up his arms, opening around the width of his biceps. Her fingers bit into his shirt and skin.

It was instinct, need, something fierce he couldn't understand, that pressed him to slam her back against the wall, take her, make her his mistress. It was so consuming to him, this passion, he was afraid if he followed it, he would break her apart. Or maybe he would break apart, feeling this—for her. With her.

Was this what his father had felt for Marissa? Was this why he'd given everything for her, everything to her? Let her slowly finish him off…so long as she kept on kissing him, looking at him, touching him like this?

When a cell phone rang, he tore his mouth away and she fumbled in a purse she'd left by the nightstand to answer. "Yes?"

His hand flicked the buttons of his shirt as she walked away and softly spoke into the receiver.

His heart rammed into his ribs, his blood a thick, terse boil in his veins. He was losing his head—and he didn't like it. He considered retiring to his study to work, put distance between them. No. No. He wanted her. He walked forward, shrugging off his shirt.

"Yes…yes, I didn't want to wake you…and yes, I'll see you…um…I'm working late and I don't know how long I'll be—" Silence. A soft, very soft, "Good night."

She came back, smiled.

"You're spending the night," he said, rendering it a statement when in fact he wanted confirmation. She was seducing him—in her pajamas, brushing her hair, staring with those green, green eyes.

Gritting his teeth against the flaring lust, he readied himself briskly, his erection springing free.

He grabbed her hand and put it on himself. If that didn't tell her, show her, how far gone he was, then he didn't know anything anymore. Still, he recalled Monterrey, all those nights with her, the days, and gruffly spoke. "You're staying the night here—with me."

She nodded and met his gaze, her eyes bright and fiery. She stroked his chest with soft, fluttering hands, dragging her lips across his jaw, his chin. "I want you in me, Marcos."

A primal hunger had overtaken his mind, his senses, until he felt as instinctive as an animal. An animal tantalized by the nearness of his mate. "You came to seduce me, didn't you? You like being at my beck and call. You came to please me, service me."

Smiling, she stepped back, and her hands went to her shirt, and Marcos watched as she began to unbutton it farther. Her fingers pulled another button free, then the next, and his eyes flicked up to hers. "I'm crazy about you," he rasped.

Virginia didn't seem to hear the truth in his words, the worry they carried. He felt out of control, and he didn't like it.

"C-can I try something with you?" she asked hesitantly, easing her top off her shoulders.

He nodded, mute with desire and anticipation.

"Would you stay still, please?" she asked.

"What are you going to do to me, Miss Hollis?" he asked in a guttural voice. He fisted his hands at his sides, watching her hands like a man about to die under them. He stood utterly still, admiring her flesh as she revealed it. His voice was barely audible, his eyes on the gentle curves of her breasts as she stepped out of her pants and at last stood as naked as he.

"Just don't move, okay?"

So he waited, his chest expanding on each breath. She trembled when she stepped closer. "Can I touch you?"

He swallowed thickly. "Please."

He sucked in a breath when she set her hand on his chest and began kissing his neck, his ear, his jaw. His breathing became a wild thing. He was motionless as her hands began to roam down his chest. She hesitated at his waist.

His jaw clamped, his nostril flared, when she wrapped her hand around him.

"Is this okay?"

Ecstasy surged through him in a tidal wave. His breath made a strange whistle. "Yes."

"Do you want—"

His head fell, forehead against hers. "Just keep touching me."

She eased her fingers between his parted thighs, to gently cup him in her palm. She began to rub.

He hurt under her stroking hand. His mind spun with images of her and him, losing themselves in his bed like he'd wanted to. His hands idle at his sides, he softly, so softly, said, "You're not pregnant, are you, *amor?*"

She tensed for a moment, and he frowned. He reached down and pried her hand away.

"Are you? We didn't use protection the first time, and I'd like to know if there were consequences."

Ignoring him, she took his shoulders in her little hands and urged him down on the mattress. "The only consequence is this, Marcos. Me. Wanting more."

He sat there, on his bed, like a man in hypnosis, and watched her straddle him.

They kissed.

Marcos was dying with pleasure, his body rocking as he feasted from her lips, lips that were soft and warm against his, lips that were wide open for his tongue to search in deep, so deep. Her sex cradled his hardness, her legs twined around him tight as her arms while he ran his hands up her sides, into her hair, groaning at the way she whimpered his name. Marcos. All he could say was, "Virginia." Oh, Virginia.

He pulled roughly at her hair.

"Why?" His voice was a cragged sound.

"I…I don't know what you're talking about."

"Why do you look at me like this? What are you playing at?"

Watching him through heavy, sooty lashes, she kissed his nipples, his abs. She was smiling—teasing him with her teeth. Her tongue. Driving him out of his mind. Out. Of. His. Mind. "Must it be a game for you to enjoy it, Mr. Allende?" she purred. "Must we play at another pretense for you to let me in?"

He snatched her hair to halt her wandering mouth, suddenly trembling with thirst for not only her body, but for something else. Something he'd always, always, seen and sensed and tried to grasp in her eyes. "Are you trying to drive me insane?" he demanded.

She pulled free and lovingly cupped his jaw, kissing him softly on the lips. "I'm trying to make you remember."

He framed her face, engulfing it between both hands, and before he took her lips in the hard, hot way his screaming soul demanded, growled, "I'm trying to *forget*."

Ten

"With luck, the negotiations will advance, then my lawyers will fly down to…" Marcos trailed off as Virginia strolled into his office the next morning, bringing those long legs with her, her raven curls bouncing with each tiny step her tapered, knee-length skirt allowed.

She stopped to check discreetly on the coffeemaker—directly in Marcos's line of vision. A bolt of lust arrowed to his groin. *Marcos, oh, please, more, more.*

Her gasps of last night echoed in his head.

This morning they'd gone at each other like—hell, like two wild animals—before they'd separately headed for the office. He'd asked her to buy something special to wear to the Fintech dinner, to splurge. She hadn't seemed to be impressed. He wanted to please her, to give her something, and yet the only thing Virginia Hollis seemed to want was him.

Damn, he was totally taken—in a way not even Marissa had taken him before. Virginia's moans, her body, writhing against his, with his. It maddened him. Heated him. Excited him. Appalled him.

Aware of the abrupt silence in the vast carpeted space, a quiet that magnified her noises as she innocently fiddled with spoons and cups, Marcos jerked his eyes back to the open proposal and tapped his Montblanc pen against the sales projection chart. He cleared his throat. "Where was I?"

"Allende. Marissa Galvez. Negotiations," Jack said, sprawling on a chair across from his desk.

"Of course." He dropped his pen and lounged back in his high-backed leather chair, stacking his hands behind his head. He met the Texan's electric-blue stare. "As soon as negotiations take on a serious note I'll call in the cavalry and we—"

Virginia leaned down to refill Jack's coffee, and her proximity to the man made Marcos's jaw clamp in anger. He felt ridiculously jealous. Yes, *diablos,* he was totally had.

"We'll close," he finished tightly, and slapped the proposal shut. She had no idea, no idea.

Or was she doing this on purpose?

The sunlight that streamed through the floor-to-ceiling windows of the Art Deco building shone over her loose hair. But she was frowning, he realized then, somehow worried, and the noose tightened around his neck.

"Miss Hollis," he said. Last night's seduction? That ridiculously simple but mouthwateringly sexy outfit? Was all this some sort of plan of hers?

She spun, shocked as if from out of her thoughts. "Yes?"

He reclined in his seat and crossed his arms. She was pale this morning. Guilt assailed him. He hadn't let her sleep much, had he? "I was telling Mr. Williams about Monterrey."

She spared a fleeting glance at Jack's lean, jeans-clad figure, and he shot her one of his disarming grins. "How nice," she said absently, and lifted the glass coffeepot to Marcos. "More coffee?"

He shook his head, searching for warm emotions in her expression, all of which usually showed on her face as she experienced them. There were none this morning either.

Her desperation last night, her need, her wanting...he'd felt them all. He'd throbbed with every one of them. Today she looked distant. Why?

I'm not Marissa...

His body clenched. No. No. She was not. Virginia was even more dangerous.

"Marissa Galvez is flying in this weekend," he then offered. Why did he offer this information? Because deep down, her words continued to pull at his heartstrings. *Mend Allende. Make it gold again.*

Did he dare? Did he even want to?

"Oh. How nice. I'm sure she'll be more agreeable this time."

The reply was so noncommittal and so lacking in generosity of feeling that he frowned. When the carved oak doors shut behind her, Jack murmured, "I see."

"Hmm?" Marcos took a long, warm gulp of coffee.

"I see," Jack repeated, propping a shiny lizard boot atop his knee.

He drank again, savoring the scent, the warmth of her coffee. Was she sick? "Mine, Jack."

"Yes, I see."

Marcos grunted. Jack wouldn't even begin to comprehend the pain of his sexual frustration. The looks she gave him— tenderness, desire, admiration, respect. When would he tire of her? He'd expected to tire within the week, and yet it had been over a month now. He could not get enough of her. Was she tiring of him? Good God, was that a possibility?

His friend's dry chuckle wafted in the air. "I assume your

plan worked with Marissa. She no doubt thought you were taken with Virginia."

Marcos pushed to his feet and headed to the wide bay window, his coffee cradled against his chest. "My bid has been rejected, Jack."

Silence.

His chest felt cramped with anger, frustration. "She controls the board and somehow made sure they declined."

"Ahh. Then I assume we're getting hostile? Why are we even discussing Allende if not?"

"We are getting hostile." He spun on his heel. "If we could."

Jack made a scratching noise. "Meaning?"

Damn Marissa and her sneaky ways. Marcos had discussed for the tenth time the purchase of her shares, and she still held off selling to him. In the back of her warped mind, she no doubt believed she could bend Marcos like she'd bent his father—who else would save her company but the son? What else would ensure her continued ownership but marriage?

No. She wouldn't get away with it, not anymore, and yet even in the midst of this surety, the fact that a woman would have power over his future made his blood boil.

"Meaning I must pressure her to sell, Williams. She's flying to Chicago this weekend—I invited her to the Fintech dinner. As long as she owns the majority of the shares, a hostile takeover is close to impossible. She must sell, and she must sell to *me*."

"Pardon my slowness, but you invited her to Chicago?"

"I want Allende, Jack."

"You want to kill it," Jack added.

Marcos absently scanned the busy sidewalks below. "And if I don't?"

Jack's usually fast retorts seemed to fail him this time.

Marcos's mind raced with every new discovery he'd made about Hank Hollis today. The man had lost his way—not unusual after the heartache of losing a beloved wife, Marcos supposed. But he'd been visiting AA meetings, seemed to be struggling to get his life back on track. He'd been a risk-taker on the job, and ruthless when it came to disciplining those beneath him. Years ago, he'd pushed his chain of stores, every single one of them, to be better, more efficient, and the admirable numbers he'd produced for them didn't lie.

"What if I told you," Marcos began, "that I'd save Allende. What if I told you I've found a man to do the dirty work— one who's driven and who's thirsty to prove something to someone?" *Maybe he'd enjoy coming to Mexico.*

"Marcos, I'm on your board as a professional, not as a friend. The same reason you're on mine."

"Of course."

And Virginia would be free of the pain her father had been causing. She would be free to be with him. Marcos.

"Well, as both, I have to tell you," his friend continued in a thickening drawl. "It's that damned prodigal apple. Any opportunity man *or* woman has to get a bite out of it, ten out of ten times, they *will*."

"Amen."

"I'm serious."

He swung around. "All right. So we get to play gods and kick them out of the kingdom. New management, new rules, no thieving, no blackmailing, no mafia."

"I agree. But who's heading new management?"

His eyebrows furrowed when he realized there was no clear space on his desk to set down his cup of coffee. The last fifteen years of his life—hard, busy years—were in this desk. A heavy oak Herman Miller, the first expensive designer piece he'd bought after his first takeover. It was old—he was superstitious—and it was a keeper and it was *packed*. The surface contained no photo frames, no figurines, nothing but a humming computer and piles and piles of papers that would later go into a roomful of file cabinets. He planted the mug over a stack of papers. "You are," he flatly repeated.

Jack's gaze was razor sharp. "Me."

His lips flattened to a grim, hard line as he nodded. "You. And a man I consider may be hungry to prove himself."

Jack hooked his thumb into his jeans pocket. "Go on."

Marcos folded into his chair, grabbed a blue pen and twirled it in his hand as he contemplated. "I negotiate for Marissa's shares and agree to allow her to stay in the company temporarily, while you and Hank Hollis will get the ropes and start a new team."

"Hank Hollis." His eyes narrowed to slits. "You're not serious."

He smiled the very same smile the Big Bad Wolf might have given Little Red Riding Hood. "Oh, but I am."

Hank Hollis would redeem himself in Virginia's eyes, right along with Allende. Marcos would make sure of it.

If Virginia had had any worries regarding her poor emotional state for the past twenty-four hours—other than having stupidly, blindly, foolishly fallen in love with Marcos Allende—she now had more proof for concern.

Pale-faced, she walked into the long tiled bathroom to stare for the twentieth time at the sleek white predictor test—the third one she'd used today—sitting next to the other two on the bathroom sink.

Pink.

Pink.

Pink.

All three were *pink*.

Of course. Because when it rained, it *poured*. Because when one thing went terribly wrong, *everything* went wrong. Because when your world collapsed on top of your head, really, *nothing* you could do would stop the crash.

Letting go her breath while the sting of tears gathered

in her eyes, she leaned back on the white tiles lining the bathroom walls and slowly, weakly, dragged her body down its length until she was sprawled on the floor.

She was very, undeniably pregnant.

With Marcos's baby.

There could be no more solid proof of her naïveté. She'd walked into his penthouse one evening with little in the way of emotional shields, without protection and without standing a chance. She might as well have torn out her heart and offered it in her hand. What had she expected would come out of it? Of all those pretend kisses, the laughter, the moments she could not forget?

Did she think he would say, "Step into my life, Virginia, I want you in it forever?"

Did she think he would say, "Marry me, *amor,* where have you been all my life?"

Oh, God. Covering her face with her hands, she considered what he would do when he found out about this.

A vision of him suggesting something bleak made the bile hitch up in her throat. She choked it back and shook her head, wrapping her arms around her stomach, speaking to herself at first, then below at the tiny little being growing inside her.

"I have to tell him." And when a wealth of maternal love surged through her, she ran a hand across her stomach and determinedly whispered, "I have to tell him."

Maybe she was more of a gambler than she'd thought. He might be furious, and he could turn her away, but still she found herself righting her hair and her clothes in front of the mirror, preparing for battle. Gathering up all the tests in the plastic bag from the drugstore and stuffing it in her purse, she once again headed back to Marcos's office.

She knocked three times. "Mr. Allende?"

His friend Jack seemed to have left already, and now, as she entered, Marcos pulled up a file from a stack on his desk, studied it, set it back down, rubbed his chin then finally stared at her.

"Close the door," he said, all somber.

She couldn't read that expression. She tried for flippant and saucy. "I'm under orders to spend a lot of money on anything I fancy."

"Are you now." He frowned. "Who is this man who orders you around? Seems to me you should run far and fast away from him, Miss Hollis."

The unexpected smile he shot her made her grin. "Did I mistakenly put whiskey in your coffee?" she asked, nearly laughing.

His eyes sparkled. "You might want to sit on my lap while you investigate."

She approached his desk, thinking about the baby, his baby, growing inside her body. "I was wondering if you were busy tonight. I'd like for us to talk."

"Virginia." He leaned forward and gently lowered her to his lap. "You have me. I'm at your disposal every night."

"Marcos…" The words *I want more* faltered in her throat.

He must have misinterpreted her concern, for Marcos dropped his hands to his sides and sighed. "Nobody knows about us, Virginia, please don't fret. I'm trying to keep things running smoothly. My office won't be abuzz with gossip, I won't allow it."

Gossip. Could everyone be gossiping? Whispering? Her stomach clenched in dread. "But you keep stealing touches and people are noticing." That much was true. And soon… how would she hide a pregnant belly?

Marcos boldly raked her figure with his gaze, reclined in his seat and said, "Then I should give these people something more to do."

She blinked, then realized he was teasing her, and she

forced her lips into a smile. But it wasn't funny. Soon they'd notice she was pregnant. Soon she'd be waddling around.

He scraped two fingers across his chin as he studied her. "You look worried."

She couldn't do this here—she felt as emotionally stable as a compass gone berserk. "Maybe the Fintech dinner isn't such a good idea," she suggested.

"It was part of our arrangement, Miss Hollis."

She swallowed and snatched up his files, deciding to postpone this for…tonight. Tomorrow. Never. "The projection room is ready."

"You have your notes?"

"Of course. And yours."

He stormed down the long hallway with her, and as people smiled at her in a "Yay, you" kind of way, her unease grew tenfold.

During the meeting, Virginia tried to concentrate on the images flicking on the projection screen. Sales charts with numbers. But Marcos sat unbearably close.

"Is it the dinner?"

She stiffened. "What?"

"Why you're worried. Is it?"

"I… No."

"The outfit? You're afraid you won't find one you like?"

She shook her head. "No."

He leaned forward. He tapped her pad. "Reading your notes here. 'Colorful charts.' Very observant, Miss Hollis. Now why are you worried? Tell me."

She attempted to take more notes but her mind was elsewhere.

"Now, you see the hedge fund study we just passed?" he said when she, apparently, was not going to talk. "We lost a little, but the fund was heavily invested in metals, as well, and the gold price has been rising, so we closed with a positive number nonetheless."

"Yes, I understand. You lose some and win some. Like… gambling."

He chuckled. "Indeed. It's all a game of risk, Miss Hollis. You weigh the benefits against the risk. And decide how to move forward. You may lose, but at least you played the game. Or you may win…and the prize is exquisite."

She did the exercise in her mind. Risk—her job, her self-respect, her body to a pregnancy, her heart…no, it was too much to bear to even think it. Benefit—save her father, who didn't deserve saving, and share a wonderful week with the most wonderful, wonderful man.

She would have liked to think that if she remained cool and aloof, she would not be risking anything. If she behaved like her usual self, there was no reason the office would speculate. If she ignored his scent, his lips and his eyes, and the fact that she'd fallen in love with him, then she could settle for the benefits. Eventually.

Except already, there was a child.

Their child.

And she wouldn't be able to hide his growing presence much longer.

Eleven

"That's supposed to be a dress?"

She sensed Marcos at the doorway, actually heard a whoosh of air as though the sight of her had stunned him, and she continued tugging the fabric down her hips, her legs, carefully avoiding his gaze as she stepped into it.

"Hello? Fintech dinner? You said buy something to dazzle them. Splurge. Buy the dress of your dreams." *Before I blow up like a balloon and have your bastard baby.*

"The key word was *something*," Marcos growled, "That is nothing."

In the middle of his spacious, carpeted closet, standing before a mirror in a satiny green dress that was making her smile and Marcos frown, Virginia flicked her hair and scoffed at his words.

His glare deepened. "I'm not taking you looking like this."

"Excuse me?"

"I'm serious."

"This is all I have, I spent a fortune on it. You told me—"

"I don't care what I said. I am saying right now, I'm not taking you…into a party with half the city…in that…that scrap."

"Don't be absurd, it's perfect."

A muscle ticked in the back of his jaw. He grabbed her arm and pulled her close. "Do you have any idea what a man thinks of…at the sight of you in that dress?"

"I thought it was elegant, but seductive, if I'd thought it was—"

He grabbed her by the waist and pressed her to him, and the shock of feeling every lean, hard inch of him against her made her gasp. "He thinks of peeling it off with his teeth. He imagines your breasts without the satin over them, and he imagines you, wrapped all around him, with your hair all across his bed."

Her bones melted inside of her.

Marcos, in a tuxedo, was easily the sexiest thing she'd ever seen. She wanted to beg him to peel the dress off her fevered body with his teeth and to wrap her limbs around him with his weight crushing her on the bed.

She tipped her face back, remembering an entire month of making love to Marcos.

In the morning. At midnight. Evenings when he got home. Coupled with those memories, she had others of him with the morning paper spread across the table, coffee cup in hand. Him shaving. Him taking a shower. With her.

She could not remember a thought that didn't make her tummy constrict.

Feeling her thighs go mushy, she stroked her fingers up his cleanly shaven jaw. "You're so handsome," she whispered.

His eyes roved her face, cataloging her flushed cheeks, the telling glaze in her heavy-lidded eyes. "I want you." His hands tightened, and she became excruciatingly aware of his erection biting into her pelvis. His eyes were so hot they were like flames. "I want you every minute of every godforsaken day and it's making me grumpy."

When she gasped, he let her go. A muscle flexed in the back of his jaw as he clenched hard. He shook his head. "Damn."

It took an effort to stand on her own two feet while quietly nursing the sting of his rejection, but she thrust her chin up with a little dignity. "This is all I have to wear."

God, she had turned into a wanton. She only wanted to touch and touch and touch him. To be kissed until her breath left her.

Flushing, she pulled open the carved-wood closet doors and began to rummage through the shoe rack.

Marcos paced the area and raked a hand through his hair. "The pearls have to go."

She straightened, a hand coming to stroke a smooth pebble at her throat. Her father had stripped out every material memory of her childhood, of her mother, the life they'd once had. He'd pawned her mother's engagement ring. The pearl earrings to match the necklace she always wore. He'd sold off the nice clothes, even the locket they'd given Virginia as a little girl.

"Are they too old-fashioned?"

"They're not you."

He pulled out a box from a drawer, and she blinked. The box was sky-blue in color, with a silken white bow on top. As his long, tanned fingers tugged the edges of the bow and the shimmering ribbon unfurled in his hand, the unmistakable words *Tiffany & Co.* appeared.

Within seconds, he'd opened a velvet box and held up the largest, most dazzling diamond necklace Virginia had ever seen. Its sparkle was blinding. Its sheer magnificence just made her breath, her brain, her everything scatter.

The piece was worthy of old Hollywood, when the women

would wear their finest evening dresses and most impressive jewels for the night. A large, oval-shaped green pendant hung from rows and rows of large, brilliant diamonds that fell like curtains and lace in the most exquisite workmanship Virginia had ever set eyes on.

"I... It's lovely."

"It's yours."

She shook her head. "I can't."

But he stepped behind her and began to fasten it around her neck. His lips grazed the back of her ear as his fingers worked on the clasp. When he was done, he turned her around to face him. "You're mine to spoil. It's yours. Tomorrow. Next week, next month, next year. It's yours."

This was him, announcing, in a way, that he was sleeping with her. No one who saw her would have any doubt. Why would he do this tonight? Why would she allow it?

She experienced a horrible urge to touch him, an even more intense one to ask him to hold her, but that would only bring the tears gathering in the back of her eyes to the forefront. She didn't understand these tears, or the desperate sensation of having lost before she'd even fought for him.

Her eyes dropped to his chest as she felt a blush creep up her cheeks. His cross lay over his chest, glinting bright gold against the bronzed skin. His breath stirred the hair at the top of her head. The warmth of his body enveloped her.

His hands framed her jaw, lifting her face to his. "I bought you earrings and a bracelet, too."

As he seized her wrist with his long, tanned fingers, she watched the thick cuff bracelet close around her. Oh, God, no wonder mistresses were always so sexy and smiling, when all their men treated them just like this!

"I can't," she still said. Because it felt so wrong. So intimate. So personal. It made her mind race with thoughts she did not—should not—think of. She was lying to him, or at least, withholding something important.

And it felt so odd, the weight of the diamonds and the forest-green emerald on her. It felt like a chain around her neck—Marcos's chain on her. And her baby. And her future.

You're mine to spoil...

"I insist, Virginia," he sternly said, and drew her at arm's length to take in the visual.

Self-conscious, Virginia dropped her gaze and tugged at a loose curl on her shoulder. The dress hugged her body like a lover's embrace, the jewels refracted thousands of little lights and for the first time in her life Virginia felt like a fraud. A woman desperate to be anyone, anyone, that the man she loved could love.

"I don't know what to say."

His chuckle was full of arrogance, but it made her melt all the same. "Then get over here."

When he drew her close and kissed her with a passion that buckled her knees and had her clinging to his shoulders, she didn't say anything at all. But her mind screamed, "We're having a baby!"

"Marcos, I'd like to talk to you, tonight."

He fixed his powerful eyes on her, his face unreadable. He seemed to have forgotten about the dress, and she wondered if he'd been jealous. Marcos wasn't surrounded by the aura of relaxation of a man who'd spent an entire night feasting on his lover, but with the tension of one who wanted more. The air felt dense between them. "I have other plans for tonight," he admitted.

She could not even smile at that. "Still, I'd like for us to talk."

He cradled her face, forced her to meet his gaze. "What is it?"

The concern in his eyes, the gentleness in his voice, only made her crave his love with more intensity. She did not want to crave it with such intensity, did not want to feel the emptiness growing inside her, realizing she lacked his love at the same time as their baby grew bigger.

Their agreement was over once she accompanied him to the Fintech dinner. And maybe they would be over, too.

She drew in a tremulous breath. "After the party."

"All right," he said, smiling. "In fact, there's something I'd like to speak to you about, too."

Inside the lavishly decorated lobby of the glass-and-steel skyscraper smack in the center in Michigan Avenue, Marcos guided Virginia through the throng of people, nodding to a few. "That's Gage Keller, he's a developer. His company, Syntax, owns half of Las Vegas now. The young woman with him is his wife."

"Second, I presume?"

He grinned. "More like sixth."

He brought her around to where a group of men and women stood by a spectacular ten-foot-tall wine fountain. "The woman drowning in jewels over there is Irene Hillsborough; she owns the most extensive collection of Impressionist art in the States. Old money, very polite."

"Very snotty?" Virginia added when the woman lifted her head to stare at her then promptly glanced away.

An appreciative gleam lit up his eyes as he smiled down at her and patted her hand. "How perceptive."

"Allende." A bearded middle-aged man Marcos had presented her to just moments ago—Samuel…something—came back to slap his back. "Haven't seen much of Santos lately. What is that troublemaker up to?"

"I wouldn't know," Marcos said with a rather bored intonation, then uncharacteristically offered, "You can ask him later if he shows." He steered Virginia away, and an immediate image of Santos—surely gorgeous and bad, so bad—made her ask, "Santos is coming?"

"If only to be a pain in the ass, yes." He said it so decidedly, so automatically, her eyes widened in surprise.

He then urged her around, and a woman with silvering hair and an ecstatic look on her face was fast winding her way toward them.

"That would be Phyllis Dyer," he continued, "the director of donations and—"

"Marcos," the woman said, lightly laying her hand on his shoulder as she kissed one cheek, then the other. Her voice quivered with excitement. "Marcos, I can't thank you enough for your generosity. I heard from the Watkinson Center for Children today and they were all wondering why the early Christmas. It was so kind of you, as usual."

Marcos gave her a curt nod. He then brought Virginia forward. "May I present Virginia."

The woman's soft gray eyes went huge. "Oh, well, how lovely to meet you. I believe this is the first time I have had the pleasure of meeting one of Marcos's girls." To her, she leaned forward to whisper, "This one's a keeper, darling, if you know what I mean."

"Oh, I'm not his… I'm actually his—"

After a bit more small talk, Phyllis left with an encouraging pat on Virginia's shoulder, and Virginia ventured a glance at him. "Why didn't you tell her I was your assistant?"

Tucking her hand into the crook of his arm, he guided her toward the sweeping arched doors that led out into the terrace. He didn't answer her.

Stepping past an elegant trellis, he led her across the terrace, illuminated with flickering gas lanterns that lined the perimeter.

When he loosened his hold on her, Virginia stepped forward and leaned on a cement banister and gazed out at the fountain. A breeze stirred the miniature trees in the nearby planters, the chilly air making her flesh pebble with goose bumps.

Unconsciously, she rubbed her arms up and down, listening to the soft piano music audible through the speakers. Somehow, the notes couldn't completely mute the faint rustle of water.

She drew in a steadying breath. "Aren't you up for a speech soon?"

Through the corner of her eye, she followed his movements as he set his wineglass on the flat surface of a stone bench. "Yes."

She gasped at the feel of his hand, warm and strong, curling around hers, tugging her forward. In a haze, she found herself slowly but surely gravitating toward him, captivated by the play of moonlight on his features and the gentle, insistent pull of his hand.

"I want us to dance, and I had a feeling you'd say no if I asked you in there."

"Dance," she parroted, mesmerized.

He smiled. Manly appreciation sparkled in his eyes as he curled his arm around her waist and pulled her even closer. *"Te ves hermosa, ven aqui."*

Anything Marcos told her in Spanish Virginia did not understand, but she felt the words so deeply, as though he were telling her a secret her instincts knew how to decode.

Both arms enveloped her and their bodies met in a visceral move, seeking a fit of their own volition. Surrounded by the piano music, feeling the cool breeze on her skin beside the fountain, Virginia suddenly wondered if she would ever experience this again. Everything. What he made her feel. The flutters inside her when she became the sole focus of those pitch-black eyes.

"Marcos," she began to protest.

"Shh. One dance."

Her involuntary squirms only made him tighten his grip on her, press her closer, urge her to move against his tall, hard body in a very slow, sensual dance. He trailed one hand up her back and delved into her hair, his fingers caressing her scalp in a light, hypnotic massage.

His hands shifted on her back, splaying wide, keeping her flat against his solid length. Virginia remembered when they had been sweaty and hot and needing each other last night. She trembled at the memory and he tightened his hold on her. She knew, sensed, felt, that he also remembered.

His eyelids drooped suggestively as he ran his knuckles down her cheek. His lips hovered over her mouth and lightly skimmed side to side. "I can't wait to take you home with me."

A feeling unlike any other bloomed inside her. She trembled down to her knees as she fought to quell it, afraid of what would happen if she set it free.

"Take me home...like a stray?" she ventured. Was this the full-moon fever? Her hormones? She'd never thought love could feel like this. So total. So powerful.

Marcos let go a rich, delicious chuckle. "More like the loveliest treasure."

She guided her fingers up his taut, hard-boned face, not daring to hope that he might...

"What is it you wanted to tell me tonight? You said you wanted to speak with me, too?"

His smile didn't fade, but a soft tenderness lit up his eyes. "Can't you guess, *chiquita?*"

"Can you give me a hint?"

He nodded, calmly explained, "It's about us."

The tender but possessive way he held her, the warm, admiring way he gazed down at her, prodded her on. "Is there...an us?"

A tingle drummed up and down her body where they touched.

His eyes went liquid, hot with tenderness as he tipped her face back. "You tell me."

I'm pregnant with your baby. She could not say it, needed to know what he had to say first.

He stroked her cheek with one knuckle. "I know what a woman like you wants," he said softly. "I can't give it to you, Virginia, but I'd like…" He trailed off when they heard a sudden noise.

Virginia's stomach tumbled with the need to hear the rest. What had he meant to say? For a single disconcerting moment, she worried he'd sensed the sudden, alarming, fragile emotions she was struggling with and this made her even more determined to hide them.

Next she heard the echoing footsteps of someone approaching. Virginia trembled when Marcos released her, her heart gripping when she spotted Marissa. Her hair streamed behind her, and her smile was provocative. And suddenly Virginia felt very small and very pregnant.

To Marcos, with wry humor, Marissa handed her arm as though he'd asked her to dance, and slyly purred, "I hope I'm interrupting something."

Bad form. Bad, bad form.

Marcos couldn't make his proposition to Virginia here. *Diablos*—where was his head? On Allende? No, it was not even there, and Marcos was shocked at the discovery.

Somewhere during the past month…somewhere between a headache, when Virginia had smoothed his hair off his brow and "knew the perfect thing to take care of that headache" for him…somewhere between one morning and another, when they sipped coffee in silence…somewhere between the sheets, when he was lost inside of her in a way he'd never thought humanly possible…somewhere between one of her million kinds of smiles…somewhere between an exchange of files…something had happened.

Marcos had let down his guard. He'd allowed himself to trust a woman, fully and completely, in a way he'd sworn he'd never trust another human. He'd allowed her to filter his mind, his thoughts, to the point where his goals had shifted… shifted and shifted until he no longer knew if they were his or hers.

"I need your help."

Marissa's soft, pleading words registered out on the terrace, and yet his eyes followed Virginia's lovely figure as she glided back into the crowded room. He'd noticed the frustration in her jade-green eyes when she stepped away, saw her struggling to hold her temper in check. She was a curious one, his Virginia. No doubt she craved to know what he'd planned to say. He smiled to himself as she wound her way away from him, into the room, her bearing as regal as a queen's.

She was wearing the most amazing, breathtaking, heart-tripping dress he'd ever seen, and he was dying to take it off her.

"Should we talk inside?" he asked curtly, shifting his attention back to Marissa, who in turn was eyeing him speculatively.

"Of course."

He led her into the decorated space. An orchestra played. Couples danced in harmony to the tune. Amongst the round tables, people mingled.

Heading toward the conference hall at the south end of the lobby, they crossed the room. He greeted several acquaintances, nodded his head at a few more and kept a close eye on Virginia. Her hair fell down to cover part of her face. Her profile was exquisitely feminine, like a doll's.

Taking in her visage, he felt a slow, throbbing ache spread inside of him, and contrary to most of the aches she gave him, this one had nothing to do with physically wanting her.

When he secured Allende, he could mend it, and he could mend her father along with it. He could give her safety and peace and pride.

The intensity with which he wanted to give this to her shocked him to his core.

Whereas before Virginia Hollis had been something to be observed but not touched in his office, a Mona Lisa behind glass, she was more real to him now than his own heartbeat. She was flesh and bones and blood. She was woman.

His fierce attraction to her, kept tightly on a leash, had spiraled out of control the moment he'd put his lips right over hers, or perhaps the moment she'd called him and Marcos had known, in his gut, he was going to have her.

Fierce and unstoppable, the emotions raged within him now, under his muscles, and the urge to cross the room and sweep her into his arms became acute.

With an effort, he tore his eyes away from Virginia, tried to steady the loud beat of his heart.

A man, notoriously tall, athletic and dark, with a smile that had been known to break a woman's heart or two, caught his attention.

Santos Allende was the only person in the world who would not wear a tie to a black-tie event. As he ambled over, he lifted a sardonic brow at the same time he lifted his wineglass in a mock toast. "Brother."

Marcos nodded in greeting, drained his drink, and introduced Marissa and Santos even though they needed no introductions. They loathed each other.

"How's the hotel business?" Marcos asked him without even a hint of interest.

"Thriving, of course."

Though Santos was irresponsible and wild, Marcos held no antagonism towards his brother, and usually regarded his exploits and antics with amusement. Except tonight he wasn't in the mood for Santos. Or anyone else.

Too smart for his own good sometimes, Santos chuckled at his side.

"So. Is that one yours?" Santos lifted his glass in Virginia's direction, and Marcos gazed at her again. His chest felt heavy and his stomach tight.

"Mine," he confirmed.

"I see." Santos smiled and rammed a hand into his pants pocket. "Mistress or fiancée?"

"Mistress," he snapped.

But his mind screamed in protest at those words.

Would she agree to his proposition to become his mistress? Live with him, be with him? She'd turned his world upside down, inside out, in over a month. He wanted her every second of the day—not only sexually. Her laugh brought on his laughter, her smiles made him smile, too. He was...he didn't know what. Enraptured. Charmed. Taken.

By her.

"That would make her your first mistress, eh, brother?" his brother asked. "No more fiancées after Marissa here."

Marissa whipped her attention back to Marcos. "You mean she's just a fling? Your girlfriend?"

He set the glass down on the nearby table with a harsh thump. "Unless you want me to leave you in prison the next time you're there, don't push it, little brother."

And to Marissa, with a scowl that warned her of all kinds of danger, "I say we've played games long enough, you and I, and I'm not in the mood for them any longer. You have something I want. The shares that belonged to my father—I want a number and I want it now."

She's his submissive, been like this for years...

Old lover demanding she be fired...competition... Allende...

Allende and Galvez...

It was easy at first, to pretend she hadn't caught bits and pieces of the swirling conversation. But after she'd heard it over and over, ignoring the comments popping up wherever she went became impossible.

It hurt to smile, and to pretend she wasn't hearing all this. But then, he'd taught her to pretend just fine, hadn't he? And she was doing quite well. Had been commending herself all evening for remembering people's names and keeping up with their conversations. And smiling her same smile.

But when the whispers were too much, she pried herself away from a group of women and strolled around the tables with her mind on escaping, finding Mrs. Fuller, Lindsay, a friendly face, but even they seemed engaged in the latest gossip.

She stopped in her tracks and frowned when a young man approached. He was over six feet tall, lean but muscled. He moved with slow, lazy charm, his smile oozing charisma. Rumpled ebony hair was slicked back behind his ears, his hard-boned face and striking features prominent. Laser-blue eyes sparkled with amusement as he halted before her and performed a mock bow.

"Allende. Santos Allende."

He spoke it the way Agent 007 would say, "Bond, James Bond," and it made her smile. So he was the elusive Santos.

"Virginia Hollis."

Drawing up next to her, he signaled with a cock of his head, a glass of red wine idle in his hand. "The bastard looking at you is my brother."

"Yes, I'm his assistant. You and I have spoken on the phone."

Santos had the looks of a centerfold, the kind that modeled underwear or very expensive suits like Hugo Boss, while Marcos had the very appearance of sin.

As if reading her mind, his lips quirked, and he added, "He didn't mention that."

"He mentioned me?"

Her eyes jerked back to Marcos; it seemed they couldn't help themselves. She always caught herself staring at him.

He was weaving toward the hallway with Marissa. When Marcos ducked his head toward her, Virginia's stomach clenched with envy and a sudden, unexpected fury.

He glanced back over his shoulder and when their gazes collided, a strange wildness surged through her. His face was inscrutable and his tuxedo was perfectly in place; only an odd gleam in his eyes spoke of his inner tumult. And in her mind, Virginia was positively screaming at him. *Everybody knows! Everybody knows I'm your stupid...silly...*

No. It was her fault, not his.

She'd wanted him, and she'd gambled for the first time in her existence. She knew his scent, the feel of his hair, the sounds he made when he was in ecstasy with her.

She knew his mouth, his whispers, knew he slept little but that he would remain in bed beside her, watching her.

She knew he liked to put his head between her breasts, knew he made a sound of encouragement when she stroked his hair.

But she did not know how to make this man love her.

This man with all these secrets, all of the locks and bolts around his heart.

He wanted Allende. To destroy it. He wanted her. To play with.

She was just his toy. Something to fool around with. Once, she might have jumped with glee. But now she wanted so much more from him, thought there could be no greater treasure in this world than to be loved by him.

"So did the affair come before he hired you or after?"

Santos phrased his question so casually and with such a playful gleam in his eyes that Virginia could only blink.

He grinned and shrugged his shoulders. "I'm sorry, I'm just terribly curious. I have to know."

Cheeks burning with embarrassment, Virginia ducked her head and tried to get away. "Excuse me."

With one quick, fluid move, Santos stepped into her path

and caught her elbow. "Marissa wants him, you do realize this?"

She stepped back, freeing her arm from his, hating that it was so obvious, so transparent on her face. "I can't see why you think I'd care."

But his curling lips invited her to mischief. "She offers something my brother wants very badly. What do you offer?"

She frowned. "I wasn't aware this was a competition—"

"It's not." He tipped her chin up, those electric-blue eyes dancing with mirth. "Because I think you've already got him."

When she hesitated, he bent to whisper in her ear, sweetening the offer with words she found she could not resist.

"My brother is very loyal, and if you managed to steal his heart…no ten businesses would top it."

But Virginia knew that one business, one woman did— when she heard the news announced later in the evening that Fintech would be taking over Allende.

Twelve

They rode to the penthouse in dead, flat silence. Marcos seemed engrossed in his thoughts, and Virginia was deeply engrossed in hers.

It took her ten minutes, while he made phone calls to Jack and his lawyers, to pack the meager belongings she'd once, mistakenly or not, left in his apartment.

She was calmer. Immobile on a tiny corner of the bed, actually, and staring at the doorway, nervously expecting him to come in any minute. But calmer.

Though she didn't know whether the nausea inside of her was due to the pregnancy or to the fact that she would not be sleeping with Marcos for the first night in over a month.

She just couldn't do this any longer. Every little word she'd heard tonight had felt like whiplashes on her back; she could not believe her colleagues would speak this way about her. And then Marcos…offering her a necklace, but not his love. Him telling his brother she was his…his…

No.

She refused to believe he would refer to her as something tacky. But the truth, no matter how painful, was the truth. Virginia was his assistant—one of *three*—and she was sleeping with her boss. It didn't matter if she'd spent the most beautiful moments of her life with him. It didn't matter that every kiss, every touch, she had given with all her might and soul. It didn't matter that she'd loved him before and loved him now.

She was sleeping with her boss, and she'd never be respected if she continued. She'd never respect *herself*.

If only she were able to tuck her determination aside for a moment and enjoy one last night with him. The last night of a month she would not ever forget. The last night with the man she had fallen in love with, the father of her unborn child.

Drawing in a fortifying breath, she left the bedroom and went searching for him.

She'd heard him in his office, barking orders to Jack over the phone, laughing with him, even—he was not concealing his delight over his deal.

The door of the study was slightly ajar, and she slipped inside in silence.

He sat behind his desk at the far end. He looked eerie behind his computer, concentrated, the light doing haunting things to his face. Her stomach clenched with yearning. "Marcos, may I talk to you?"

He stiffened, and his head came up. Her breath caught at the devastating beauty of his liquid black eyes, and her heart leapt with a joy that quickly became dread when he remained silent. There was lust in those orbs, desire, and she seized on to that with all her might before he jerked his gaze back to the computer. "I'm very busy, Virginia."

She tugged at the hem of her dress, uneasy of how to proceed. She tried to sound casual. "Marcos, I thought we could discuss…something. I may not spend the night and I really feel it's important—"

"Jesus, do we have to do this now?" His hands paused on the keyboard, then he dropped his face and rubbed his eyes with the heel of his palms. "I'm sorry. Right. Okay. What is it, Virginia?"

Her eyes widened at his condescending tone. The thought that he'd always put Allende and his business before her made her stomach twist so tight she thought she would vomit. She'd forgotten she was his plaything. If she produced money maybe he'd give her five minutes now?

"We were going to discuss…us." Her voice trembled with urgency. "At the dinner, you mentioned wanting to say something."

He leaned back, his expression betraying no flicker of emotion, no hint of what was going through his mind. "Can't us wait a day? Hmm?"

"No, Marcos, it can't."

He sat up straighter, linked his hands together, and kept silent for what felt like forever. His calm alarmed her. He was too still, too composed, while his eyes looked…indulgent. "What is it you want to say to me?" he at last asked.

Suddenly she felt like young Oliver Twist, begging, "Please, sir, I want some more." And she hated him for making her feel like that.

Her voice broke and she swallowed in an attempt to recover it. "Look, I realize what kind of arrangement we have," she began. "A-and maybe it was good for a time. But things change, don't they?"

He nodded, his entire face, his smile, indulgent.

She dragged in a breath, trying not to lose her temper. "Marissa, Marcos."

"What about Marissa?" His eyes were so black, so intense, she felt as though they would burn holes through her.

Are the rumors true? she wondered. *Did she force you*

*into a marriage bargain only so you could once again own
Allende?* "You loved Marissa. Do you love her still?"

A frustrated sound exited his throat as he flung his hands
over his head. "I'm not discussing Marissa now, of all times,
for God's sake!" he exploded.

But Virginia plunged on. "I think it very tacky to jump
around from bed to bed, don't you?"

His eyebrows drew low across his eyes, and he nodded.
"Extremely."

To her horror, her throat began closing as she pulled her
fears out of her little box and showed them to him. "She hurt
you, and maybe you wanted to use me to hurt her back—"
Why else would he want Virginia? She was not that smart,
not that special, not that beautiful, either!

She tried to muffle a sob with her hand and couldn't, and
then the tears began to stream down her cheeks in rivers.
With a muffled curse, he rose and came around the desk,
walking toward her. His face and body became a blur as he
reached her, and though she tried to avoid his embrace, her
back hit the wall as she tried escaping.

He bent over her, wiped her tears with his thumb. "Don't
cry. Why are you crying?"

The genuine concern in his voice, the soul-wrenching
tenderness with which he cradled her face, only made the
sobs tear out of her with more vigor. "Oh, God," she sobbed,
wiping furiously at the tears as they streamed down her
face.

When he spoke, he sounded even more tortured than she
was. "Don't cry, please don't cry, *amor.*" He kissed her cheek.
Her eyelashes. Her forehead. Her nose. When his lips glided
across hers, she sucked in a breath of surprise. He opened his
lips over hers, probed her lightly with his tongue, and said,
in a tone that warned of danger, "Please give me ten minutes
and I'm all yours. Please just let me…"

When he impulsively covered her mouth, she opened for

the wet thrust of his tongue, offering everything he didn't ask for and more. His kiss was hot and avid, and it produced in her an amazing violence, a feeling that made her feel fierce and powerful and at the same time so vulnerable to him.

The possibility that he was feeling some kind of pity for her made her regain some semblance of control. She pushed at his wrist with one hand and wiped her tears with the other. "I'm all right."

"You're jealous." He took her lips with his warm ones, nibbling the plump flesh between words. "It's all right. Tell me that you are."

She shook her head, not trusting herself to speak.

"I was when you danced with Santos," he rasped, "jealous out of my mind. Out. Of. My. Mind." His teeth were tugging at her ear, and he was making low noises of pleasure as his hands roamed up her sides, following her form, feeling her.

She dragged her mouth across his hair, softly said, "I can't do this anymore, Marcos."

He froze for a shocked moment.

In one blindingly quick move, he lifted her up and pressed her back against the wall, pinioning her by the shoulders. "Is this your idea of getting my attention?"

Her heart thundered in her ears. "I can't do this any longer. I want more." *A father for our child. A man who'll always stand by me. Someone who cares.*

A nearly imperceptible quiver at the corner of his right eye drew her attention. That was all that seemed to move. That and his chest. Her own heaving breasts. They were panting hard, the wild flutter of a pulse at the base of his throat a match to her own frantic heartbeat. "What more do you want?" His voice was hoarse, more a plea than a command.

She grasped the back of his strong neck and made a sound that was more frustrated than seductive. "More! Just more, damn you, and if you can't figure out it's not your money then I'm not going to spell it out for you."

He stared at her as though what she'd just said was the worst kind of catastrophe. Then he cursed in Spanish and stalked away, plunging his hands into his hair. "You picked the wrong moment to share your wish list with me, *amor*."

"It's not a long list," she said glumly. She felt bereft of his kisses, his eyes, his warmth, and wrapped her arms tightly around herself. "We said we'd talk, and I think it's time we did."

"After midnight? When I'm in the midst of closing the deal of my life?"

"I'm sorry about the timing," she admitted.

She swallowed hard for some reason, waiting for him to tell her something. He didn't. His back was stiff as he halted by the window. His breaths were a frightening sound in the room—shallow, so ragged she thought he could be an animal.

But no, he wasn't an animal.

He was a man.

A man who had ruthlessly, methodically isolated his emotions from the world. She did not know how to reach this man, but every atom and cell inside of her screamed for her to try.

But then he spoke.

"Virginia." There was a warning in that word; it vibrated with underlying threat. It made her hold her breath as he turned. There was frustration in his eyes, and determination, and his face was black with lust. "Give me ten minutes. That's all I ask. Ten minutes so I can finish here and then you'll get your nightly tumble."

His words jerked through her, one in particular filling her with outrage. *Tumble!*

She began to quake. A chilling frost seemed to seep into her bones.

Stalking around her, he fell back into his chair, was sucked back into his computer, and began writing.

"Tumble," she said.

He set down the pen and met her gaze. The man was mute as wallpaper.

She signaled with trembling fingers. "For your information." She wanted to fling her shoe at his face, to shred every single paper on the pile she'd neatly organized atop his desk, but she clenched her eyes shut for a brief moment. "I do not want a tumble!"

Several times, Virginia had imagined how their parting would be.

Not even in her nightmares had she imagined this.

She couldn't bear to be in the same room with him, didn't dare glance up to make note of his expression.

Stricken by his lack of apology, she choked back words that wanted to come out, hurtful things she knew she would regret saying, words about being sorry she'd met him, sorry she loved him, sorry she was pregnant by him, but staring at the top of his silky black hair, she couldn't. Instead she said, "Goodbye, Marcos."

And Marcos…said nothing.

Not *goodbye*. Not *chiquita*. Not *amor*.

But as she waited by the elevator, clutching her suitcase handle as though it was all that kept her from falling apart, a roar unlike any other exploded in his study. It was followed by an ear-splitting crash.

The clock read 1:33 p.m.

He had what he wanted, Marcos told himself for the hundredth time. Didn't he? And yet the satisfaction, the victory, wasn't within reach. Perhaps because what he really wanted was something else. Someone else.

The pressure was off his chest—the lawyers were currently sealing the deal. Allende for a couple of million. Marcos now owned every single share of stock in the company, had recovered every inch and centimeter and brick and truck of what Marissa had taken from him.

It had not taken much at all to bend her to his will; the woman had nothing to bargain with. Marissa had to sell or she'd go bankrupt. She'd held no more attraction for him, as she'd thought, no temptation. After a few harsh words from him and a few tears from her, there had finally been a bit of forgiveness between them.

And with that, everything had changed. By her admittance to defeat, she'd unwittingly granted Marcos the opportunity to color his past another shade that wasn't black.

He felt...lighter, in that respect. But heavy in the chest. So damned heavy and tortured with a sense of foreboding he couldn't quite place.

"You needed me, Mr. Allende?"

His heart kicked into his rib cage when Virginia strolled into his office five minutes after he'd issued the request by phone.

Yes, I need you. I do. And I'm not even ashamed to admit it anymore.

Dressed in slimming black, she held a manila file in her hand, and a few seconds after she closed the doors behind her, Marcos spoke. "You left before the ten minutes were over."

Silently she sat and fiddled with her pearls, her eyes shooting daggers at him when she spared him a glance. "I realized you wanted your space, so I indulged you."

Those last words came barbed, as though he'd once spoken them in sarcasm and she were flinging them back at him. She looked tired, his Miss Hollis, he noted. As though she'd slept less than an hour and tossed around for all the rest. Like he had.

He didn't understand her anger very well. But they'd had plans to speak afterward, had been sleeping together so delightedly he hadn't expected the loss of her last night to affect him like it had. Were ten minutes too much to ask?

"Ten minutes, Miss Hollis. You can't even grant me that?"

"You were being—" As though offended by her own thoughts, she bolted upright in the chair, spine straight. "Something of a jerk."

He choked. "Jerk! This spoken by an opinionated little brat I've spoiled rotten?"

The blow registered in her face first, crumpling her tight expression. Marcos raked his fingers through his hair and shot up to pace his office.

He felt like celebrating with her, like marking this momentous day in his career with something even equally outstanding for him personally. But somehow he sensed he had to make amends with her first.

Virginia had wanted him last night. First, he'd been occupied with Marissa. Who'd deceived and lied to him. And who had become so insignificant in his life, he'd forgiven her. After he got what he wanted from her.

All this, thanks to Virginia.

Suddenly, Marcos felt a grieving need to explain, to placate her, to restore the sparkle in her pretty green eyes. Staring around his office, at the papers scattered across the desk, he quietly admitted, "Virginia, I want to make you a proposition."

Her slow and deep intake of breath was followed by a dignified silence. This was not the way he'd intended to ask her and yet suddenly he had to. Here. Now. Had to know she would belong to him, only him.

They were fighting, the air between them felt electric, charged with anger and lust and something else he couldn't quite place. Something fuzzy and warm that made him feel close to her even when she annoyed him.

He strode over to her chair and bent, put his palm on her

bare knee, and said, with fervor, "Would you be my mistress, Virginia?"

The way she automatically breathed the word *no,* he'd have thought he'd slapped her. Her eyes shone with hurt and her mouth parted as though she wanted to say something else but couldn't. "No," she said again, on another breath, this one made of steel.

"I don't think you understand what I'm saying," he said gently, stroking her knee and moving his hand up to clasp hers where it rested on her lap.

"Don't!" She said it in such a fierce voice that he halted. Even his heart stopped beating. She shook her curls side to side, her face stricken. "Don't touch me."

What was this? What was this?

He caught her face in one hand, his heartbeat a loud, deafening roar in his ears. "Darling, I realize you might have misinterpreted my interests in speaking to Marissa, which I assure you were only business. It's you I want, only you. And I'm very prepared to give you—"

"What? What will you give me?" She stood up, her eyes shooting daggers at him. "Do you even realize that the only thing I've been pretending all this time is that I don't love you?"

His heart vaulted, but his voice sounded dead as he stepped back. The confession felt like a bomb dropped into his stomach. "Love."

She chose to look out the window. And at last handed him the file. "Here's my resignation."

She set it atop his stacks and started for the door, and Marcos tore across the room like a man being chased by the devil. He caught her and squeezed her arms as his paralyzed brain made sense of her words.

"If you're telling me you love me," he said through gritted teeth, "look at me when you say it!"

She wrenched free. "Let go of me."

He caught her elbow and spun her around, and she screamed, *"I said don't touch me!"*

Worried the entire floor may have heard that, he let go of her. His chest heaved with the cyclone of feelings inside of him. He curled his fingers into his hands and his fingers dug into his palms, his knuckles jutting out.

"You want me," he growled.

"No." She backed away, glaring at him.

"You tremble for me, Virginia."

"Stop it."

"You want me so much you sob from the pleasure when I'm inside you."

"Because I'm *pretending* to enjoy your disgusting *tumbles!*" she shot. She was flushed and trembling against the wall, her nipples balled into little pearls that begged for his mouth. But in her voice there was nothing but pain.

"Pretend? When the hell have we pretended?" He crushed her against him, squeezed her tight even as she squirmed. "We're fire, Virginia. You and I. Combustion. Don't you understand English? I'm asking you to stay. With me. And be my mistress," he ground out.

Did she even realize he'd never in his life said this to a woman before? When her lashes rose and her gaze met his, the damaged look in her eyes knocked the air out of him. He didn't expect the slicing agony lashing through him at her next words.

"I'm not interested in being your mistress."

When she disengaged from him and pulled the doors open, he cursed under his breath, raked a hand through his hair. All noise across the floor silenced, and he immediately grabbed his jacket, shoved his arms into it as he followed her to the elevator.

He pushed inside before the doors closed, and she turned her face toward the mirror when he demanded, "Do I get two weeks to convince you to stay? I want you here. And I want you in my bed."

"You want. You need." Her voice quivered with anger, and its tentacles curled around him so hard he could've sworn it would kill him. "Is that what you wanted to speak to me about? Becoming your...*mistress?*"

His heart had never galloped this way. His plans had never veered off so unexpectedly, so decidedly. Their gazes met. Hers furious. His...his burned like flames. He grabbed her shoulders. The need inside him was so consuming he saw red. "Say yes. Christ, say yes now."

But the way she looked at him wasn't the same way she always did. "Do you think that's what I want?" she asked, so softly he barely heard through the background elevator music. "Did I ever give you the impression I would...settle for...such an offer?"

Stunned that she would look at him like he was a monster, he took a step away from her, and another. His body burned with the want to show her he meant not to punish but to love her with every graze of his lips and every lick of his tongue.

And he said, out of desperation, impulse, the exact second the elevator halted at the lobby floor, "I love you."

And the words, magic words, ones he'd never, ever said before, didn't have the effect he'd predicted.

Her laugh was cynical. "See, you're so good at pretending, I don't believe you."

And she spun around and walked away, out of the elevator, away from him, away from it all.

Stunned, he braced a hand on the mirror, shut his eyes as he fought to make sense of the rampaging turmoil inside him.

What in the hell?

Thirteen

Alone in his Fintech offices, motionless in his chair, Marcos stared out the window.

The nineteenth floor was empty. It was 3 a.m. But there was no power on this earth, no way in hell, that he'd go back alone to his apartment. His penthouse had never felt so cold now that Virginia Hollis was gone. The sheets smelled of her. He'd found a lipstick under the bathroom sink and he'd never, ever felt such misery. The sweeping loneliness that had accompanied that unexpected find was staggering.

He'd stormed out of his home and now here he was, inside his sanctuary. The place where he evaluated his losses and plotted his comebacks. Where he'd conquered the unconquerable and ruthlessly pursued new targets. Where, for the last month, he'd spent countless hours staring off into space with the single thought of a raven-haired temptress with pale, jade-green eyes.

And now he stared out the window, blinded to the city below, and he told himself he did not care.

He told himself that a month from now, he would forget Virginia Hollis.

He told himself this was an obsession and nothing more. He told himself the gut-wrenching, staggering throb inside him was nothing. And for the hundredth time, until the words rang true and his insides didn't wince in protest every time he thought them, he told himself he did not love her.

But it was a bluff. A farce. A lie.

Virginia had her money. Their arrangement had culminated at the Fintech party and had left him with an overwhelming sense of loss he couldn't quite shake. She'd left him wanting. Wanting more.

Marcos, I love you.

She hadn't said it in exactly those words—but in his mind, she did. And he'd never heard sweeter words. More devastating words. Because suddenly, and with all his might, he wanted to be a man who could love her like she deserved.

The pain in her eyes—he'd been the one to put it there. Touch of gold? He scoffed at the thought, thinking he destroyed anything he touched that had life. He'd put that misery in Virginia's eyes and he loathed himself for it.

His proposal, what he'd offered her, not even half of what he'd truly wanted from her, sickened him.

All along, he'd wanted her. He was a man accustomed to following his gut, and he did it without a conscience. He knew when he saw land and wanted it. He knew what he looked for when he bought stocks. He knew, had known from the start, he wanted Virginia in his bed, under his starved, burning body. But now, clear as the glass before him, he knew what else he wanted from her.

He wanted it all.

He wanted a million dances and double that amount of her smiles.

He wanted her in his bed, to see her when he woke up, to find her snuggled against him.

He wanted to pay her credit card bills and he wanted her with a baby in her arms. His baby. His woman. His *wife*.

Mia. Mia. Mia.

He'd been alone his entire lifetime, pursuing meaningless affairs, convincing himself that was enough. It had all changed. Slowly, almost imperceptibly, but surely, ever since the day he'd hired Virginia Hollis.

Now he had broken her heart before she'd truly admitted to having lost it to him. He should've treasured it. Tucked it into his own and never let it go.

Sighing, he pushed his chair around and stared across his office. A dozen plasma TV screens hung on the wall to the right. They usually enlivened the place with noise and light, but were currently off. They lent a gloom to the area that Marcos found quite the match to his mood.

In fact, a morgue was quite the match to his mood.

He stalked outside, and made his way to a sleek wooden desk. Her items were still on it. He scanned the surface—polished to a gleam, all orderly, all her, and he groaned and let his weight drop into her chair.

Her rejection felt excruciatingly painful. Not even the day Marissa Galvez had stared up at him from his father's bed had he felt such helplessness.

What in the devil did she want from him?

As he stroked a hand along the wood, he knew. Deep in the closed, festering pit of his emotions, he knew what she wanted. Damn her, she'd been playing him for it! Seducing him, delighting and enchanting him, making him love and need and cherish her.

And now he couldn't even remember why he had thought she didn't deserve everything she wanted. Because she was a woman, like Marissa? Why had he thought his bed would be enough for everything she would lack? Had he grown so heartless that he would rob her of a family?

He began opening and closing the desk drawers, looking for some sign of her. Something—anything—she might have left behind.

For the first time in his life, someone else's needs seemed more important than his, and he loathed the overwhelming sense of loss sweeping through him like an avalanche.

If he had an ounce of decency in him, if he was not the unfeeling monster she thought him to be at this moment, Marcos would let her go.

And just when he was certain it was the right thing to do, just when he was determined to forget about her and all the days they'd pretended and all the ways they'd been both wrong and right for each other, he spotted the boxes crowded into the back of her bottom drawer.

And the three test strips. All of them had the same result.

"Nurse, is my father out in the hall?"

Virginia had been transferred to a small private room in the west hospital wing, where she'd slept for the night hooked up to an IV drip, and this morning the one person she longed to see hadn't yet made an appearance. She wanted to go home already—she felt tired, cranky, lonely—and still the nurse kept delaying her departure.

The balmy-voiced nurse fidgeted around the bare room, organizing the trays. "I believe he's outside. I'm sure he'll come in shortly."

Virginia sighed, the sensation of having been run over by an elephant especially painful in her abdomen and breast area. She cupped her stomach. Amazing, that the baby already had its heartbeat. Amazing that just as she left its father, the baby had tried to leave her body, too.

"Virginia?"

She went completely immobile when she heard that.

There, wearing a severe black turtleneck and slacks, stood Marcos Allende in the doorway. Her heart dropped to her toes. She felt the urge to snatch the sleek red carnation her father had set on the side table and hide her pale, teary face behind it, but she was too mesmerized to pull her eyes away. Large, hard, beautiful—Marcos's presence seemed to empower the entire room, and she suspected—no, knew—everyone in this hospital must be feeling his presence.

He stood with his feet braced apart, his arms at his sides, his fingers curled into his palms. And something hummed. Inside her. In her blood, coursing through her veins.

"An acquaintance, miss?"

The nurse's tone gave a hint of her preoccupation. Did she feel the charge in the air? Was the world twirling faster? The floor falling?

Virginia nodded, still shocked and overwhelmed by this visit, but as she stared at the sleek-faced, long-nosed young woman, she hated her mind's eye for gifting her with another, more riveting image of Marcos's dark, cacao gaze. His silken mass of sable hair. Long, tanned fingers. Accent. Oh, God, the accent, that thick baritone, softly saying *Miss Hollis*...

"I'll leave you two for a moment, then."

Oddly close to being devastated, Virginia watched the nurse's careful departure, and then she could find no excuse to stare at the plain white walls, no spot to stare at but Marcos.

If she had just been torpedoed, the impact would have been less than what she felt when he leveled his hot coal eyes on her. He stood as still as a statue.

Why didn't he move? Was he just going to stand there? Why didn't he hold her? Why was he here? He was angry she quit? Angry she hadn't collected her items? Did he miss her just a little bit?

She sucked in a breath when he spoke.

"I'm afraid this won't do."

The deep, quiet, accented voice washed over her like a waterfall. Cleansing. Clear. Beautiful.

Oh, God. Would she ever not love this man?

She pushed up on her hands, glad her vitals were no longer on display or else Marcos would know exactly how hard her heart was beating. "Marcos, what are you doing here—"

He looked directly at her as he advanced, overpowering the room. "I had to see you."

She sucked in breath after breath, watching him move with that catlike grace, his expression somber. Her body quaked from head to toe. The unfairness of it all; he was so gorgeous, so elegant, so tempting. So unreachable. And she! She was so…so beat-up, tired, drained. Hospitalized. Oh, God.

Her lips trembled. As if she weighed next to nothing, he bent and gently scooped her up against him, and Virginia liquefied.

I almost lost our baby, she thought as she wound her arms around him and buried her face in his neck.

He inhaled deeply, as though scenting her. Then, into her ear, his voice ringing so low and true it tolled inside of her, "Are you all right?"

Only Marcos could render such impact with such softly spoken words. Her entire being, down to her bones, trembled at his concern. And then came more. It was just a breath, whispered in her ear, and he whispered it with fervor.

"I love you."

Her muscles clenched in protest, and her head swiveled to her father's when she spotted him at the open doorway. The weathered man's face was inscrutable and his suit was perfectly in place; only the ravaged look in his eyes spoke of what he'd done.

He'd told Marcos about the baby?

"You lied to me, you left me, and yet I love you," Marcos

continued, his voice so thick and gruff, as though he were choking.

After the fear, the cramps and the possibility of losing her baby, Virginia had no energy. She just wanted him to speak. The sturdiness of his hard chest against hers gave her the most dizzying sensation on this earth. She'd thought she'd never feel his arms again and to feel them around her, holding her so tight, was bliss.

She didn't realize she was almost nuzzling his neck, breathing in his musky, familiar scent, until her lungs felt ready to explode.

"Do you think we could pretend," he whispered into the top of her bent head, "the past two days never happened, and we can start again?"

More pretending? God, no! No more pretending.

But she refused to wake up from this little fantasy, this one last moment, refused to lift her face, so instead she rubbed her nose against the side of his corded neck. A strange sensation flitted through her, like the soaring she felt when she played on the swings as a child.

His voice was terse but tender as he wiped her brow with one hand and smoothed her hair back. "And our baby?"

Shock didn't come close to what she experienced. Her nerves twisted like wires. "P-pardon?"

"You lost our child?"

For the first time since Marcos had come through that door, Virginia noticed the red rimming his eyes, the strain in his expression. Even his voice seemed to throb in a way she'd never heard before.

She moved not an inch, breathed no breath, as her mind raced to make sense of his question. Then she glanced out the small window, not at what lay beyond, just at a spot where Marcos's face would not distract her. "What makes you say that?" she asked quietly, her fingers tugging on themselves as she scanned the room for the possible culprit behind this misunderstanding. Her father.

"Look at me." Marcos's massive shoulders blocked her view as he leaned over the bed rails. His breath stirred the top of her head as he scraped his jaw against her hair with absolutely no restraint, and then he spoke so passionately her middle tingled. "Look at me. We'll have another baby. I've always wanted one—and I want one with you." He seized her shoulders in a stronghold, his face pained and tortured as he drew away and forced her to meet his gaze. "Marry me. Today. Tomorrow. Marry me."

"I— What do you mean *another* baby?" After many moments, she pinned Hank Hollis with her stare. "Father?"

Wide-eyed, her father hovered by the opposite wall, shifting his feet like an uncertain little boy. He opened his mouth, then snapped it shut, then opened it again, as if he were holding on to great words. "I told him you'd lost the baby."

She gasped. What a horrible thing to say! "W-why? Father! Why would you do that?"

The man rubbed the back of his neck, pacing the little room. "So he'd leave. You said you didn't want any visitors."

While the honest words registered in her foggy mind—the first protective thing her father had done for her in ages—Virginia stared at the aging man. Her heart unwound like an old, twisted shred of paper.

For years, she had been so angry at this man. Maybe if she hadn't changed, become pregnant, fallen in love, she'd still be. But now—she didn't want resentment or anger. She wanted a family, and she'd take even one that had been broken.

Virginia leveled her eyes on the beautiful, thick-lashed cocoa ones she'd been seeing in her dreams and straightened up on the bed, clinging to that fine, strong hand. "Marcos,

I'm not sure what he told you, but I'd like to assure you I'm all right. And so is the baby."

When she pictured telling Marcos about a child, she hadn't expected an audience, nor having to do it in a hospital room.

Still. She would never, in her life, forget this moment.

Marcos's expression changed, metamorphosed, into one of disbelief, then joy. Joy so utter and pure it lit his eyes up like shooting stars.

"So we're expecting, then?"

The term *we* coming from his beautiful mouth made her giddy with excitement.

He smiled, and it was brilliant, that smile, that moment.

Did this please him? Yes! She'd bet her life on it.

She nodded, her heart fluttering madly, a winged thing about to fly out of orbit. "I'd like to go home now," she admitted, and although her father stepped forward to offer assistance, the words weren't meant for him.

She gazed up at Marcos—quiet and mesmerizing—as she eased out of the hospital bed with as much dignity as she could muster.

His attention was no longer hard to bear. She wanted it; she wanted him.

Virginia Hollis knew this man. Inside and out, she knew him. How true he was to his word. How dedicated. How loyal. And how proud. She didn't need any more proof than his presence here, his touch, the look in his eyes and the promise there.

Rising to her full height, she linked her fingers through his and squeezed, feeling flutters in her stomach when he smiled encouragingly down at her. "Yes, Marcos Allende. I'll marry you."

Epilogue

The day arrived three months before the baby did.

Walking up to the altar, with the music shuddering through the church walls, Virginia had eyes only for the dark, mesmerizing man at the far end of the aisle. Tall and smiling, Marcos stood with his hands clasped before him, his broad shoulders and solid arms and steely, stubborn jaw offering love and comfort and protection.

Virginia was certain that nobody who watched him would be blind to the way he stared at her. Least of all she.

They shared a smile. Then her father was letting go of her arm.

Soon Marcos was lifting the flimsy veil to gaze upon her face and into her eyes, eyes which she used to fervently tell him, *I love you!*

Their palms met, their fingers linked, and the moment they did he gave her a squeeze. She felt it down to her tummy.

I, Virginia, take thee, Marcos, to be my lawfully wedded husband…

When he spoke his vows, the simplest vows, to love and cherish, her eyes began to sting. By the time the priest declared them man and wife, she was ready—more than ready—to be swept into his arms and kissed.

And kiss her he did. The priest cleared his throat. The attendants cheered and clapped. And still he kissed her.

Virginia let herself take her first relaxed breath once they were in the back of the limo. Gravitating toward each other, they embraced, and tiny tremors of desire spread along her torso and limbs. She'd had this fool idea of waiting to be together again until they married—and she was dying for him to touch her.

As they kissed, Virginia found her husband already dispensing with her veil. "There we go," he said contentedly. "Enjoy the dress because I assure you, it is coming off soon."

Actually relieved to be without the veil and anxiously looking forward to Marcos dispensing with the dress, she leaned back on the seat and cuddled against him. "I never knew these things were so heavy," she said. The skirt ballooned at her feet but thankfully there was no volume on top to keep her away from the man she most definitely intended to jump at the first opportunity.

"Come here, wife." He drew her close as the limo pulled into the street and the city landscape slowly rolled past them. Staring absently outside, Virginia sighed. His arms felt so good around her, being against him so right. Being his wife.

Both protectively and possessively, Marcos pressed her face to his chest and with his free hand, reached out to rub her swelling stomach. She'd noticed the more it grew, the more he did that. "How is my little girl today?" he asked against her hair.

Her eyebrows drew into a scowl. "We're having a boy,"

Virginia countered. "A handsome, dashing boy like his daddy. No girl would kick like this little guy does, trust me."

"Your daughter would, you saucy wench," he said with a rolling chuckle. "And my instincts tell me we are having a plucky, curly-haired, rosy-cheeked daughter. She'll run my empire with me."

Virginia smiled against his chest and slid a hand up his shirt to find the familiar cross lying at his throat and play with it. "Father keeps asking how many grandchildren we plan to have, he's obsessed with wanting it to be at least three."

Marcos laughed, and that laugh alone warmed her up another notch.

"Ahh, darling," he said. "He can rest assured we'll be working on that night and day." The praise in his words and the suggestive pat on her rear filled her with anticipation of tonight and future nights with her complex, breathtakingly beautiful, thoroughly giving and enchanting husband.

"He's so changed now, Marcos," she admitted, feeling so relaxed, *so* happy.

"His work in Allende has been impressive, Virginia. Even Jack is amazed."

"And you?"

He snorted. "I got to say to the moron 'I told you so.'"

She laughed. Then she snuggled closer and said, "Thank you. For believing that people can change. And for forgiving that little fib he told you at the hospital."

He nuzzled the top of her head. "He was trying to protect you—he didn't know me yet, and I respect that. Your father deserved a second chance, Virginia. We all do."

She sighed. "I'm just glad he's put all his efforts into making the best of it. And I'm proud of you, dear sir, for being wise enough to put the past behind you and keep Allende."

And for being most decidedly, most convincingly, most deliciously in love with her.

* * *

The band played throughout the evening, and the guests at the reception laughed and danced and drank. Hardly anyone would notice the groom had kidnapped the bride, and if they did, Marcos sure as hell didn't care.

He still could not understand why Virginia had gotten it into her head to play hard-to-get leading up to the wedding, and even less could he comprehend why he had obediently complied.

But now in the cloaked shadows of the closet, he had Virginia right where he'd always wanted her. In his arms. His mouth feasted on her exposed throat while his hands busily searched her dress for access—any access—to the smooth, creamy skin beneath.

"Careful!" Virginia screeched when he yanked on the delicate zipper at the back and an invisible button popped free.

He laughed darkly and maneuvered through the opening. "You're not wearing it again, *reina*. I could tear it apart and dispense with all this silliness." The guests had been crowding them for hours when all Marcos wanted was to be with his bride. Now his hands stole in through the opening at the small of her back, where he instantly seized her cushy rear and drew her up against him. "Come here. You've been teasing me all night."

"How kind of you to notice."

"Hmm. I noticed." He kissed the top of her breasts, all evening looking lush and squeezable thanks to Christian Dior, and then used his hands to gather the volume of her skirts and yank most of them back.

She automatically wrapped her stockinged legs around him when he pressed her against the wall. "You're incorrigible," she said chidingly, but he could hear the smile in her voice and the little tremble that said how very much his wife wanted to be ravaged by him.

He brought his hands up front and lowered them. "I'm open to being domesticated."

"Luckily I'm open to attempting that daunting task. In fact—no, not the panties!" A tear sounded, Virginia gasped, and his fingers found what they were looking for.

"Bingo," he purred.

"Oh, Marcos." Slipping her hands under his jacket and around his shoulders, she placed fervent little kisses along his jaw. "Please."

With a rumbling chuckle, he found her center and grazed it with his fingers. "Please what, *chiquita?*"

Against his lips, she mumbled, "You know what, you evil man."

"Please this?"

"Yes, yes, that." She left a moist path up his jaw and temple, and in his ear whispered, "I was aching to be with you all day."

"Shame on me." He turned his head and seized her earlobe with his teeth, tugging. "For keeping you waiting."

"I adore what you do to me."

He groaned at the husky quality of her voice. "No more than I, darling." Unable to wait, he freed himself from his trousers and, grasping her hips, began making love to her.

A whimper tore out of her, and she clutched his back with her hands.

"Chiquita." He wound his arms around her and was in turn embraced and enveloped by her silken warmth, completely owned and taken by the woman who had single-handedly stolen his heart.

No matter how quiet they tried to be, they were groaning, moving together. Marcos closed his eyes, savoring her, his wife and partner and mate and woman. When she exploded in his arms with a gasp, crying out his name into his mouth, he let go. Gripping her hips tighter, he muttered a choked, emotional *te amo* then let out a satisfying, "Hmm."

"Hmm," she echoed.

Inconspicuous minutes later, the bride and groom exited the closet. The ballroom brimmed with music and laughter, most of the guests who remained being the people closest to them.

With an appreciative eye, Marcos noticed the bride looked deliciously rumpled. Her cheeks glowed bright, and the fancy hairdo she claimed had taken endless hours to achieve had become magnificently undone.

As if reading his thoughts, she shot him a little black scowl. "I'm sure that everyone who sees me now will know—" she rose up to whisper into his ear "—that you just tumbled me in the closet. Really. Is that how your wife should expect to be treated, *Señor* Allende?"

Smiling into her eyes, he lifted her knuckles to his lips. "My wife can expect to be treated with respect and admiration and devotion."

With a dazzling smile, she let him drag her to the dance floor when a compellingly slow song began. "I believe this dance is mine," he said, and meaningfully added, "So is the one afterward."

She stepped into the circle of his arms, finding her spot under his chin to tuck her head in and sliding her arms around him. "You are a greedy fellow, aren't you?"

His lips quirked, and his eyes strayed toward the arched doorway, where his little brother stood, barely visible through the throng surrounding him. "With Santos around, I don't plan to let you out of my sight."

Virginia laughed. "He's already told me everything. Even about the time you broke his nose and chin. I swear that man loves to make you out as the ogre." She glanced past her shoulder and wrinkled her little nose. "Besides, he seems pretty busy with the two he brought tonight…and the dozen others he's trying to fend off."

Grateful that for the moment the guests were oblivious

to them as they danced amidst so many familiar faces, Marcos ran a hand down her back and glanced at the firm swell between their bodies. "How do you feel?" he asked, somber.

She smiled as she canted her head back to meet his gaze. "I feel...perfect." She kissed his lips and gazed up at him with those same green eyes that had haunted him. Their sparkle surpassed the blinding one of the ring on her finger, and her smile took his breath away—like it did every day. "You?" she asked.

His lips curled into a smile, and he bent his head, fully intending to take that mouth of hers. "A hundred thousand dollars shorter," he baited. He touched her lips, and his smile widened. "And I've never felt so lucky."

* * * * *

COMING NEXT MONTH

Available August 10, 2010

#2029 HONOR-BOUND GROOM
Yvonne Lindsay
Man of the Month

#2030 FALLING FOR HIS PROPER MISTRESS
Tessa Radley
Dynasties: The Jarrods

#2031 WINNING IT ALL
"Pregnant with the Playboy's Baby"—Catherine Mann
"His Accidental Fiancée"—Emily McKay
A Summer for Scandal

#2032 EXPECTANT PRINCESS, UNEXPECTED AFFAIR
Michelle Celmer
Royal Seductions

#2033 THE BILLIONAIRE'S BABY ARRANGEMENT
Charlene Sands
Napa Valley Vows

#2034 HIS BLACK SHEEP BRIDE
Anna DePalo

REQUEST YOUR FREE BOOKS!

2 FREE NOVELS
PLUS 2
FREE GIFTS!

Passionate, Powerful, Provocative!

SDESI0R

HARLEQUIN®

A Romance

FOR EVERY MOOD™

Spotlight on
Heart & Home

Heartwarming romances
where love can happen
right when you least expect it.

See the next page to enjoy a sneak peek
from Harlequin® American Romance®,
a Heart and Home series.

Five hunky Texas single fathers—five stories from Cathy Gillen Thacker's LONE STAR DADS *miniseries. Here's an excerpt from the latest,* THE MOMMY PROPOSAL *from Harlequin American Romance.*

"I hear you work miracles," Nate Hutchinson drawled. Brooke Mitchell had just stepped into his lavishly appointed office in downtown Fort Worth, Texas.

"Sometimes, I do." Brooke smiled and took the sexy financier's hand in hers, shook it briefly.

"Good." Nate looked her straight in the eye. "Because I'm in need of a home makeover—fast. The son of an old friend is coming to live with me."

She was still tingling from the feel of his warm palm. "Temporarily or permanently?"

"If all goes according to plan, I'll adopt Landry by summer's end."

Brooke had heard the founder of Nate Hutchinson Financial Services was eligible, wealthy and generous to a fault. She hadn't known he was in the market for a family, but she supposed she shouldn't be surprised. But Brooke had figured a man as successful and handsome as Nate would want one the old-fashioned way. *Not that this was any of her business...*

"So what's the child like?" she asked crisply, trying not to think how the marine-blue of Nate's dress shirt deepened the hue of his eyes.

"I don't know." Nate took a seat behind his massive antique mahogany desk. He relaxed against the smooth leather of the chair. "I've never met him."

"Yet you've invited this kid to live with you permanently?"

"It's complicated. But I'm sure it's going to be fine."

Obviously Nate Hutchinson knew as little about teenage

HAREXP0810